Office of Scientific Operations - Release #6

K McConnell

Published by K McConnell, 2024.

OFFICE OF SCIENTIFIC OPERATIONS - RELEASE #6

First edition. May 15, 2024.

ISBN: 979-8230632634

Written by K McConnell.

The Office of Scientific Operations

With the conclusion of the traumatic events in 1933 surrounding the shocking affair involving the city of New York and a beast commonly referred to as "King Kong" the President of the United States, Franklin Roosevelt, established the Office of Scientific Operations (OSO). The purpose of the OSO was to monitor, evaluate the level of risk and assist in any manner the mitigation of danger of any and all scientific operations and anomalies. With the rapid pace of scientific discovery this office was given the highest priority and clearance to investigate any potential threats or consequences to the interests of the United States of America.

These are the untold stories of actual events. The cinematic interpretations have concealed the real stories. Those stories are presented here.

Declassified file: #174

Commonly referred to by the public as "The Werewolf".

1956

1

Marcus Edmonds, Director of the Office of Scientific Operations, pushed some silver hair back from his forehead while he stared down at the open file folder laying on the conference table in front of him. He was a stocky man and had been the Director of the Office of Scientific Operations, the OSO, for many years now. It was a stressful job. The responsibility was huge and he felt it every day.

It was the OSO's job to investigate any phenomena that might pose a risk to the safety and security of the United States. Not from foreign powers. Ike had a good handle on dealing with that stuff. It was the stuff that came from elsewhere. From the ever growing realm of science and these days that seemed to be coming at an increasing pace.

But the OSO was not restricted to just investigating such things. They were tasked with helping in any way they could with negating, diminishing or eliminating the threat as well. That was the truly hard part for the OSO agents. It put them in very real danger on virtually every mission.

There was a knock on the conference room door. Marcus lifted his head and saw Agent Elliot Simms looking through the glass side panel next to the door. Marcus waved at Simms to come in. Simms was the Chief Investigator for the OSO.

"Sir?" Simms said. "You wanted to see us?"

"Yes. Please." Marcus waved towards the chairs around the table.

Robbie Regan followed Simms into the room. Both Simms and Regan sat down. Simms, dark haired and serious, and Regan, blonde and smiling waited for Marcus to speak.

Marcus slid the file folder over to Simms. "I am sending the two of you to Vermont."

"Vermont?" Regan asked. "Somehow it doesn't seem like Vermont would be on the front line of any crisis."

"Where is Mountain Crest?" Simms asked looking up from the file.

"In the north of Vermont." Marcus said.

"Ah, northern Vermont in December. Lovely." Regan commented.

"This only really talks about a murder in Mountain Crest. We...generally don't focus on something..." Simms' voice trailed off.

Marcus nodded. "Right. Something local law enforcement would handle. The circumstances of this may warrant our interest. The Surgeon General has asked me to look into this."

"The Surgeon General?" Simms asked.

"A friend of mine. It seems that an old friend of his, a doctor in Mountain Crest, by the name of Gilchrist contacted him. Apparently, the murder victim in this particular case was killed by...something." Marcus said looking a little uncertain about what he was referencing.

"Something?" Regan asked. "That sounds ominous."

"There seems to be some uncertainty as to whether the killer was human or something else." Marcus said.

"Something like...what?" Simms asked.

"That, gentlemen, is what you two are going to find out. In addition, I have some concern about the location." Marcus said.

"Vermont?" Regan asked.

"Not far from Mountain Crest are two scientists doing undefined biological research outside the oversight of the government. We have been keeping tabs on them, but we are not sure what they have been working on. I do not like the coincidental nature of this mysterious murder and the proximity of these unsupervised scientists." Marcus explained.

"I see." Simms said nodding. "Look into this murder and check if there is any connection to these scientists."

"Yes." Marcus.

"Sounds easy enough." Regan said.

Simms glanced over at Regan.

"Right." Regan said. "It somehow never works out that way."

With no direct flights from Washington DC to Montpelier Vermont Simms and Regan were forced to fly into New York and catch the single daily flight to Montpelier. In Montpelier they were provided a car from local law enforcement and they headed north following the directions the Montpelier police gave them.

"Why do I get the feeling we are heading towards uncomfortable beds and limited food choices." Regan said glancing around at the rugged mountainous terrain they had been steadily winding their way deeper into over the last hour.

"Well, its not a vacation." Simms said.

"It could be if you were into skiing." Regan said. There was at least a foot of snow covering nearly everything as they gained some elevation.

"I think its the next road up here." Simms said waving towards the windshield.

Regan turned on to a road that was a mix of snow and gravel.

"Not much out here." Regan said after they had driven about a mile up the road.

"Probably why they chose this place." Simms said setting the file folder of the two scientists aside.

"Yeah." Regan agreed. "Oh, there's something. Looks like just a house."

"I think its their place. Yeah, that's the address. Stop here." Simms said. "Let's watch the place for a few minutes."

They sat there quietly for a few minutes.

Regan shifted and pulled an ID badge out of his pocket. "Let me look at this thing again. So, let's see, we're from the Department of Agriculture looking into some missing veterinary grade anesthesia. Hmm, you think they'll buy that?"

Simms shrugged. "Probably not. I'm sure no matter who we said we were they would be suspicious. Doesn't matter. We'll take a look around whether they object or not."

They sat for a while longer, but nothing stirred at the house.

"I say we go take a look." Regan said.

Simms nodded. "Agreed. There's no car here so I suspect they're not here right now. Let's find out."

They got out and walked the short distance to the house. At the front door they knocked and waited. No answer. No sounds. Simms reached out and tried the door knob. Locked.

Without saying anything Simms pointed past Regan indicating for him to go left and then gestured that he would go around the right side of the house.

Regan hesitated. He patted the left side of his coat while looking at Simms.

Simms shook his head. "No guns." He said quietly.

With a nod Regan headed off to the left of the house. Simms eased around right. There was the faint sound of a hum, but it was unclear where it was coming from.

As Simms moved past the back corner of the house he spotted Regan at the other end of the house. They exchanged looks and it was obvious that neither one had seen anything of interest. As they both moved further along the back of the house an odd small debris field came into view in the snow.

Regan and Simms stopped at the mess in the snow. It was apparent that it had come from the shattered window at the back of the house. Without saying anything Simms pointed at the splintered wood mixed in with the broken glass.

Regan nodded. Whatever went through the window was not only strong enough to break the glass, but also destroy part of the window frame itself. Regan waved a hand back away from the back of the house.

Simms followed Regan's gesture. It took a moment to recognize that beyond the debris was some kind of trail in the snow.

Regan took a step towards the snow plowed trail, but Simms waved him back. He pointed at the house. He wanted them to check the house out first. Regan came back and the two of them peered in through the broken window.

Inside was a room filled with a variety of equipment, but the room looked like it had been hit by a tornado. There was stuff strewn everywhere and much of it was smashed.

Simms hesitated and then decided going in through the shattered window was just as easy as walking all the way back around the house in order to kick the front door in.

"Let's go in here." Simms said.

"Seems like whoever or whatever was here is gone now." Regan said.

"Agreed." Simms said. He hoisted himself up on to what was left of the lower part of the window frame. A moment later he rolled himself into the room. Regan did the same.

"Wow. Somebody did some serious redecorating." Regan said.

"Whoever it was it appears they were really unhappy with this place." Simms said. He knelt down and studied some of the broken equipment. He thought he recognized some of it, but other parts and pieces were too small or crushed to determine what it came from.

There were the remains of several cages scattered about along with some blood splattered around.

"Ugh." Regan said.

"What?" Simms asked turning towards Regan.

Regan pointed over in a corner. "There's a rabbit's head over there. I don't think the head is lucky is it?"

Simms scooped up some papers that were scattered about the floor and started looking through them. "I don't think so."

"Ah." Regan said lifting up a filing cabinet that had been partially tipped over. "There's a live rabbit here in a cage."

"Leave it." Simms said staring at the papers in his hands. "We'll have a crew come in and go more thoroughly through this stuff. They can deal with it."

"Shit." Regan said. "That thing is feral. It snarled at me and tried to bite through the wire."

"A rabbit?" Simms asked glancing over at Regan.

"A carnivorous rabbit, I guess." Regan said.

"I don't think they come in that variety." Simms said casually.

"This one does." Regan said staring down at the cage.

"I'm going to try to find a phone and call this in." Simms said. He walked out of the wrecked lab.

Regan wandered back over to the window they had climbed through. He studied the window frame carefully. He took a step back and stared for a moment longer and then turned and walked out of the lab. He could hear Simms' voice from a front room of the house.

"Yes sir. We'll push on to Mountain Crest and see what we can learn there." Simms said as he hung the phone up.

"We're done here?" Regan asked.

"Yeah. A clean up crew is on its way here to sort this all out." Simms said nodding.

"Before we go come take a look at something." Regan said walking back into the lab.

Simms followed Regan to the shattered window frame.

"What does that look like to you?" Regan said pointing at several locations around what was left of the window frame.

Simms leaned a little closer and then stood up. He glanced over at Regan.

"Claw marks." Simms said.

"My thought too." Regan said with a nod. "Big claws."

"Hmm." Simms said. He glanced over at the snarling rabbit and then back at Regan.

"Yeah." Regan said.

2

"Its not too much further to Mountain Crest from here." Simms said as they turned at a crossroad.

"That's good because I am getting——what the hell?" Regan said slamming on the brakes and turning the wheel sharply to the left.

A black blur streaked out from the left side of the road. One moment there was nothing but endless pines trees on both sides of the road and then suddenly something black and fast was in the road directly in front of them. With incredible speed the thing bounded off into the trees to their right.

The car skidded some on the snowy road and came to a stop.

"What the hell was that?" Regan said.

"Don't know." Simms said as he was yanking the car door open.

Regan leaped out of the car and circled around to join Simms. They both had their .45s out and their eyes searched the forest in front of them. They knew the thing———whatever it was———could not be far away, but the woods were weirdly quiet.

"Well?" Regan asked.

Simms waved at the shoulder of the road. "There's a track over there. Come on."

The two of them started working their way through the snow alongside the road following what was clearly the tracks of the thing that had leaped in front of them. They had gone about 20 yards before Simms stopped. Both of them were breathing hard from working their way through the foot deep snow.

"I don't think we're going to catch up with this thing." Simms said through deep breaths.

Regan nodded. "Yeah. Its obvious that thing isn't having as much trouble moving through this snow like we are."

"Any ideas what it was?" Simms asked looking over at Regan.

Regan shook his head. "No. It was hairy. Not sure if it was on four feet or two."

"Had to be on four feet. Nothing on two feet can move like that. But..." Simms hesitated. "...I thought I saw it wearing..."

"Pants?" Regan looked over at Simms.

They looked at each other for a moment.

"Yeah." Simms said. "Kind of like pants."

"Most four legged creatures don't wear pants." Regan said staring off into the forest around them.

Simms shook his head. "I'm not aware of any. We're losing daylight."

"Yeah." Regan said as the two of them turned back towards the road and their car.

It didn't take them much longer to reach the outskirts of the small town of Mountain Crest. Simms pulled the car into a parking spot along the street. They walked a short distance to a nicely lit diner which seemed like a beacon as the dark of the evening descended. They sat down at a table and ordered a couple of coffees.

"So, what's the plan from here?" Regan asked.

"We still need to find those two scientists. That's our top priority here." Simms said taking a short sip of coffee.

"Assuming they are still alive." Regan commented.

Simms glanced up from his coffee at Regan.

Regan shrugged. "That lab was in pretty bad shape."

Simms nodded slightly. "Yes, but, no blood. At least, not enough to suggest two men were killed there. I don't think they were there when the lab was destroyed."

"Yeah, well, that does suggest that there might actually be something worse here than two rogue scientists." Regan said.

"Yeah, but we knew that was a possibility." Simms said.

"Well, yes, but I really was hoping, you know, for once, to just prove the trouble was just some misunderstanding and not have to find some kind of monster running around." Regan said.

"Like that ever happens." Simms said.

"Shh!" An old man in the booth next to theirs turned around and held a finger in front of his lips.

"I'm sorry. Were we being too loud?" Regan asked politely.

The man wore an old fedora that had been through many better days than this one. He had gray stubble on his wrinkled face and his suit kept the bedraggled theme going.

"You shouldn't be talkin' about it." The man said quietly and glancing carefully around the diner.

"About..." Simms started.

"The Werewolf." The man said in a frightened hushed tone.

Simms and Regan exchanged uncertain looks with each other. Was the guy crazy or...

"The Werewolf?" Regan asked.

"Yeah. The monster you said that's runnin' around here." The old man's head nodded at them.

"Its a Werewolf?" Regan asked.

The old man waved at them. "Keep your voice down. It could be anybody."

"Sorry." Regan said. He glanced across at Simms' skeptical face. "How...do you know its a Werewolf?"

"The doctor, in Mountain Crest, he said some kind of animal is doing the killin'." The old man said.

"So, like maybe a mountain lion or a plain ordinary wolf could be the cause of all of this." Simms said casually.

"No. No." The old man insisted. "They've seen it."

"Who saw it?" Regan asked.

"Some people." The old man answered.

"Yes, but who, specifically?" Simms asked.

The old man half shrugged. "I don't know who they were. But some people seen it. They said it was walking on two legs."

Again Simms and Regan exchanged a glance.

"You said it could be anybody? So you think its someone from Mountain Crest?" Regan asked.

The old man shrugged. "No one knows. Like I said, could be anybody." The old man waved a hand in the general direction of the rest of the diner's patrons. He turned back around.

"Do you think—-" Regan started, but Simms held a hand up. Regan recognized that it was too public here to discuss it any further. They paid for their coffees and headed back out to their car.

3

As they approached the main part of Mountain Crest there was road block across the main street. Simms and Regan had to wait a moment for the car in front of them to be cleared before they could pull up to the officer. Simms rolled his window down and handed his ID to the officer.

"What's this?" The officer said staring at the ID.

"Uh, my ID." Simms said.

"What's the...Office of Scientific Operations?" The officer asked. He studied them suspiciously.

"Maybe you should call that in and have it checked out." Simms suggested.

The officer seemed even more suspicious. "I don't need you to tell me what to do." He stood there awkwardly for a moment. Clearly he wasn't sure if he would get in more trouble for not calling this in or if he did call it in.

"I'll...just call this in." The officer moved slowly back to his car parked behind him across the road. As usual it took a few minutes for the officer to get some kind of confirmation. He walked back to their car. This time he seemed less suspicious and more hesitant.

"Sorry, sir. I guess you can go...well, anywhere you want." The officer said slowly. He leaned forward and looked across the front seat at Regan with a questioning look. Regan held his ID out. The officer quickly stood up.

"Right." The officer quickly stepped back and waved them on.

They drove past the road block and on into the center of Mountain Crest. Simms parked along the curb and they walked over to a small hotel and checked in. Coming back out of the hotel they crossed the street to a restaurant. They ordered dinner as the last light of the sun disappeared. After dinner they sat drinking a cup of coffee.

Regan leaned over towards the window and looked up. He sat back up. "Looks like its a full moon out there."

"You mean the kind that turns people into werewolves?" Simms asked with a hint of sarcasm in his voice.

Regan smiled. "Not really what I was thinking, but a full moon does afford for reasonable light—-especially on a snowy mountainside."

Simms nodded. "I was thinking along similar lines. You think we could pick up the trail of whatever that was we saw on the drive here?"

Regan gave a shrug. "Maybe. Beats sitting around here all evening."

Simms nodded again. "Agreed."

The lane on the main road leading out of Mountain Crest was not being stopped by the police. There was a steady stream of people that had decided not to wait and see who might be killed next.

Simms and Regan drove past the road block and on down the road. They passed the diner they had stopped at earlier and retraced the miles back to where they had seen something run across the road in front of them. It wasn't easy in the eerie white twilight of a full moon to recognize where the incident occurred. They stopped a couple of times only to climb back into the car and keep going when they realized it wasn't the right spot. Finally they were sure and pulled the car over on to the narrow shoulder of the road. They got out, stood and looked around. It was very quiet. Peaceful and, actually, quite beautiful. Snow covered mountain forest in the glow of the bright white moon.

Simms waved towards the slope leading up from the road. "Well, I am thinking we see if we can pick up the trail."

"And if we can't?" Regan asked.

Simms gave a quick shrug. "Maybe we just climb to the ridge top and see if that gives us any clue on where to go from there."

Regan nodded. "Sounds like as good a plan as any."

They moved up the sloping forest in silence for while. A couple of times they thought they had come across some tracks, but after a short distance the tracks either disappeared or they lost faith that they were following the genuine tracks of any animal. They kept going up.

Above them the ridge line dipped down and was closer to them than the rest of the ridge which rose on both their left and right up to higher peaks. Breathing heavily they reached the ridge top. So far they had seen no indication of any animals skulking about.

They stood for a moment on the ridge top catching their breath. The other side of the ridge sloped down into a narrow valley. The valley had long ago been cleared and there was, clearly visible in the moonlight, a homestead of some kind below them. A light in the window of the house suggested someone lived there. From this distance they couldn't make out too many details of the place.

"Wonder if those people have seen anything." Regan said.

"Worth checking out." Simms said and with a nod they both began descending towards the farm in the valley.

They were about half way down the slope to the farm when Regan, slightly ahead of Simms, pulled up. He stood still. Frozen.

"What?" Simms asked.

Regan held up a hand. They both stood quietly.

"You hear that?" Regan asked.

At first Simms heard nothing and started shaking his head and then stopped. There was something. He concentrated.

"Is that crying?" Simms asked.

"I thought that too, but I'm not so sure now." Regan answered.

The sound got a little louder.

"Someone in trouble?" Simms asked.

Regan shook his head slightly. "Not sure that's a person."

"We better get down there." Simms said and they started moving faster down the slope trying not to slip or stumble in the snow or forest debris.

They had gotten much closer when Regan stopped again.

"What?" Simms asked.

"That's not a person. I think its livestock. Sheep maybe." Regan said.

Simms listened. "I think you're right. They don't sound happy."

"No." Regan said shaking his head.

They moved only a short distance further when they heard a scream. They stopped again and looked at each other.

"That wasn't a sheep." Simms said.

"No. Pretty sure that was a woman." Regan said.

They were now close to emerging out of the dim light of the forest and into a gently sloping field that led down to the farmhouse and several surrounding buildings. Behind one of the buildings was a sizable corral and numerous sheep.

Just as the two of them burst out into the open field they heard the sound of a car start and then the scuffling sound of tires kicking up gravel. They watched as a car tore down the long and winding driveway.

They stood watching the car for a moment. The scream of a sheep tore their attention back to the corral. With a quick look at each other they both drew out their .45s and started running towards the corral. It took them a couple of minutes to reach the corral by which time they were down to a weary jog.

They looked past the fence around the corral. The sheep were all at the far end, furthest from Simms and Regan and well away from the barn. The sheep were clearly in a panic, pushing and shoving one another against the far fence.

To their right most of the corral was bathed in moonlight. To their left was the single story barn casting about an eight foot shadow out in to the corral. Simms and Regan were watching the sheep trying to determine what was scaring them.

Suddenly, to their left, in the shadow of the barn, something moved. It had gone unnoticed as just a dark shape among several dark undefinable shapes in the shadow of the barn. But this shape grunted and stood up. At its feet was a black and white pile of something. It took Simms and Regan only a moment to recognize that the black and white pile was a sheep that had been torn apart.

"What the...?' Regan started to say.

Simms swung his .45 around towards the moving shape. "Stop!"

The shape moved with amazing speed. With one bound it was speeding away from them in the shadow of the barn.

Simms fired, but the shape had long since vacated where Simms was aiming. The bullet smacked into the barn.

Regan reacted and fired after the retreating dark shape. His shot too hit nothing more than the wood siding of the barn.

A moment later the shape burst out into the moonlight, but at that distance it was still difficult for Simms or Regan to make out much detail. The sheep scattered in wailing panic as the thing moved towards them and in a smooth easy leap it cleared the far fence.

Simms and Regan climbed over the fence and raced across the corral. When they reached the far side where the thing had exited the corral Regan started climbing over the fence. Simms reached out and stopped Regan.

Simms shook his head. "There's no way in hell we are going to catch up with that thing."

Regan hesitated and glanced out towards the forest a short distance away from the fence. He looked back at Simms and slid back down to the ground.

"Yeah. I guess you're right." Regan said.

They walked back to the dead sheep. They squatted down next to it.

"Holy crap. That thing's been shredded." Regan said.

Simms nodded. “Definitely. This...takes some sharp instruments and...a lot of strength.”

“Or claws.” Regan said.

Simms sighed. He ran a hand across his forehead pushing back some hair. “Or claws.”

They climbed back out of the corral and slowly, with guns still out and an occasional glance behind them, made their way back up the slope of the ridge. They were moving more slowly now. Partially because they were a little worn out from the rush to get down to the farm, but more so out of an abundance of caution now. It would take them about an hour at this pace for them to get back to their car and it was going to be a long hour in the darkness of the forest, knowing that there was indeed something very dangerous in Mountain Crest.

4

Regan sat in the restaurant and stared out at the main street of Mountain Crest. The morning light was casting a slight orange glow across the town and the snow of the surrounding mountainside.

Regan was half way through his morning cup of coffee when Simms joined him at the table.

“What did the boss say?” Regan asked.

“The Director has altered our priorities.” Simms said. The waitress came over and poured Simms a cup of coffee.

Regan sighed. “Knew that was coming.”

Simms nodded. "Yeah. Priority one now is hunting down whatever this thing is that's terrorizing these people. After that we can track down our missing scientists."

"Great." Regan said. "So any idea on exactly how we're going to catch that thing?"

Simms shook his head slightly. "Unfortunately, no. I think all we can do is to head back up to that farm and see if we pick up some tracks."

Regan looked skeptical. "At the speed with which that thing moves it could easily crisscross all over these hills. It could take us weeks to find it."

"I know." Simms said staring down at his coffee. "I am open to a better plan."

"Seems like it might be time to talk to the sheriff here and see what his plan is. I heard some people hear saying something about the sheriff setting out some traps for the thing." Regan said.

Simms nodded. "I was planning on catching up with the sheriff this morning and try to coordinate our efforts."

When they had finished breakfast Simms and Regan walked out of the restaurant and headed down the sidewalk in the direction of the police station. They had made only half way to the station when two officers came out of the newspaper office as Simms and Regan were passing. One of them was the sheriff.

"Sheriff?" Simms asked stopping in front of Sheriff Haines.

Haines stared at Simms for just a moment. "What?" Haines' voice was abrupt and he seemed annoyed at the question.

Simms pulled out his ID and held it up for Haines to read. Haines glanced down at it. He looked expressionless at Simms.

"I got a call last night about some government guys being here. Someone in Washington told me to cooperate with you." Haines said.

"Well, that's what we wanted to—-" Simms started.

"I don't need any help from any government guys. We'll handle this ourselves." Haines said. Haines started to walk past Simms.

"If this is what it appears to be, some kind of dangerous creature on the loose, things could go badly very quickly." Regan said.

Haines turned slightly and looked at Regan. "I told you. We'll handle it." Haines walked away.

Simms just stared at Haines as he walked away.

"Well, that went well." Regan said.

"Yeah." Simms said.

They stood there for a moment longer.

"So. Off to the farm?" Regan asked.

Simms nodded. "Looks like that's today's plan."

They had to get some directions to the farm. Since they didn't know an address or the owners of the farm at all it took some explaining to determine whose farm that was. In the end, it came down to agreeing it was the farm that the woman came into town last night screaming of a monster attacking her sheep. That equated to the "Winslow's place". With few roads cutting through these mountains they still managed to miss the turn to the Winslow's farm and had to turn around. When they arrived there, little had changed from the previous night. The owners had not returned and the slaughtered sheep was still laying next to the barn.

They circled around the corral making their way towards the far side where they had last seen the creature vault the fence and disappear into the forest. Along the way they looked for other signs that the creature may have returned during the night, but found nothing.

When they reached other side of the corral they were able find prints in the snow of something. It looked like a very large dog footprint, but clearly the prints were from a two legged creature.

"Up that way somewhere." Simms said pointing up the tree covered slope in front of them.

"Yeah." Regan said and they started up the slope. As they reached the edge of the forest they exchanged a look and together drew their .45s out.

They hiked up the mountainside for about 20 minutes occasionally spotting a print to confirm they were still roughly following the path the creature had taken the night before. They stopped to catch their breath. The snow made each step a slippery adventure.

"Are you sure these will stop that thing?" Regan held his .45 up.

"No." Simms answered. "But, did you want to carry something heavier up this mountain?"

"Hmm. Good point." Regan said. They continued on for a little while, but their progress was getting slower. Part of that had to do with the fact that they were getting tired, but the closer they got to the ridge top the more the terrain became rockier. There were no tracks on the bare rock and they were having more difficulty following the tracks.

"You know I almost miss dealing with a giant monster rampaging through a city. At least the ground is flat in the city." Regan said as they stood breathing heavily and standing on a large rocky outcropping.

"Yeah." Simms said. He was about to say something else and then froze.

Regan recognized Simms sudden tenseness and looked around at the trees nearby. He didn't see anything and then he heard it. It was some distance away from them.

Regan looked at Simms. "What...was that?"

"Not sure." Simms said.

The sound came again, but a little closer.

"Sounds sort of like a wolf, I guess." Regan said.

Simms frowned. "More like a dog."

"That's a weird sounding dog if it is." Regan.

Simms nodded. "Agreed. And...big."

"Yeah." Regan said staring off in the direction the sound was clearly coming from now. "You think that's our friend?"

Simms shrugged. "Don't know. The tracks go that way." Simms pointed to his right.

"And the sound...is that way." Regan said pointing in the opposite direction.

"Yeah." Simms said.

"So, which way?" Regan asked.

The sound came again, but closer still.

Simms waved a hand for Regan to squat down. "Let's wait for this thing." Simms whispered.

They crouched low, guns ready and stared down the mountain into the forest. They didn't have to wait long. Regan pointed. Simms stared and then spotted it. There were a number of trees obscuring their view so it was not possible from where they were to get a good look at it.

Regan and Simms glanced at each other. Regan edged closer to Simms so they could whisper.

"What is it?" Regan asked softly.

Simms shook his head. He held up his free hand and wiggled his fingers mimicking a person walking on two legs. He shook his head. Regan nodded. While they couldn't see what it was very well it was obvious that this thing was moving on four legs.

Simms waved at Regan to follow him as he slowly climbed off the rock outcropping down to get closer to the thing. They had hardly started moving when the creature stopped and stood frozen. Simms froze too and Regan followed suit.

The creature, for a moment, seemed to turn a little in their direction and both Regan and Simms tensed up. Then, with a snort the thing turned back and faced down the mountain. They could tell the creature was sniffing the air. In an instant the thing bounded down the slope through the trees.

"Can you see it?" Regan asked in a whisper.

"No. It went down." Simms answered quietly.

"The sheep." Regan said.

"Right. Let's see if we can get down there while it is occupied with the sheep." Simms said. He stood up and started making his way down the mountain as quickly as the slippery slope and caution would allow him to. Regan followed closely behind.

They had moved quick enough to find that they had actually nearly caught up to the creature. It had stopped at the edge of the forest and was sniffing the air. They still could not get a clear look at it. They had come to a stop at what seemed like a safe distance from the thing and there was some trees and brush interfering with their line of sight.

Another moment passed and then the thing bounded out of the forest and into the open. It crossed the short distance to the corral in a heartbeat.

Simms and Regan moved as fast as they could to the edge of the forest. They both stopped several steps out into the open space. They stared at the creature that was much more visible now. They watched as the thing cleared the fence in an easy leap. Within seconds it had snatched a sheep and then in several bounds reached the far side of the corral. Again it easily cleared the fence in a leap—-with its prize.

"Holy shit." Regan said.

"Yeah." Simms said.

"I saw it, but...I'm still not sure what I was seeing." Regan said.

"It...looked like a dog." Simms said, still staring into the distance where the thing had disappeared into more forest beyond the other side of the corral.

"They don't make dogs that big. That thing must have been 6 foot at the shoulder." Regan said.

Simms nodded. "Yeah."

"I don't thing the bears up here get that big." Regan said. He too stared off into the distance.

Simms sighed and shook his head. "I...don't think that's the thing we were tracking."

"Damn." Regan said. "I was thinking that too, but I just didn't want to say it. What the hell is going on up here?"

"Don't know." Simms said. "But if we find any more of these things up here we are going to need to call in some military help on this."

"I'm not opposed to doing that right now." Regan said.

"Well, before we do that let's try to catch up to one of these things and see what one of these will do to it." Simms said lifting up his .45.

They circled around the corral and began following the tracks of the creature. These tracks were easier to follow. They went through snow and four legs made much more of a discernible trail. Especially with regular splotches of blood.

They followed the trail for a while knowing that the creature was easily making better time up the slope and through the forest than they were.

"What's that?" Regan said pointing ahead of them.

They climbed a little higher up the slope and stopped.

"Oh." Regan said as they stared down at it. "I guess that was part of a sheep."

"Yeah." Simms said stepping carefully around the bloody pile.

They reached the top of the ridge. The bloody tracks crested the ridge and continued on down to their left. They stood there for a minute catching their breath. They were about to start down the slope in the direction of the tracks when a sound from below stopped them. It was from somewhere down the slope, but to their right.

"That sounds like a person." Regan said.

Simms nodded. "Through a bullhorn, I think."

"Yeah." Regan agreed.

They listened for another minute.

"It...sounds like someone's name." Regan said tilting his head.

"Duncan...Marsh...?" Simms glanced over at Regan.

Regan nodded. "Yeah. That's what it sounds like. So, what do we do? Follow the voices or the creature?"

"Well, who ever is making the noise could potentially be drawing our friend," Simms pointed at the bloody tracks at their feet, "in their direction. We might better find those people and warn them."

Regan nodded again. "Yeah. Probably so."

They moved to their right. They could hear someone calling to "Duncan" and acknowledging that he was hurt. It didn't mean anything to them, but as they got close and heard sounds of movement below Simms waved for the two of them to stop.

"Let's see what's going on before we get closer." Simms said in a whisper.

They listened while someone was imploring "Duncan" to show himself so they could help him. Then someone named Helen began calling to Duncan. From somewhere just below where they crouching they saw some movement and then a child's voice calling out "Dad".

Simms and Regan looked at one another and exchanged shrugs. They slowly edged down closer to get a better view of what was happening. They saw a man laying on the ground attended by a couple of people and a woman and a boy moving further down the slope. After a few minutes a couple of people helped the man on the ground up and slowly limp down the mountain.

When the group had moved far enough down the mountain Simms and Regan stood up.

"Not sure what that was." Regan said.

"Don't know." Simms said.

"You think that guy was injured by the thing we were following?" Regan asked.

Simms shook his head. "I don't think so. We've been following that thing since it was beyond the farm on the other side of this ridge." Simms waved a hand towards where they had come down from.

"Yeah." Regan agreed. "That thing was fast, but not that fast."

Simms glanced back up the mountain. "I don't think we are going to catch up with that thing today. Let's head back down to town. Maybe we can find out about whatever went on here. See if it has anything to do with the creatures that seem to be running around out here."

"Good." Regan said. "I wasn't looking forward to hiking back up there."

"Can't say I was either." Simms said. "But...the car is parked over at that farm."

"Shit." Regan sighed. "I forgot about that."

Slowly the both of them began trudging back up the slope.

5

"So, you're sure that's what the guy said?" Simms asked.

Regan nodded. "Yeah. Everyone's talking about it. The sheriff has this 'werewolf' locked up in a cell."

Simms sighed. "Somehow there are still some dots that are not connected in this."

Regan nodded. "Yeah. What did the Director have to say?"

Simms shifted his weight as he leaned against the corner of a building in the chilly dark of the evening.

"He said they sent a team up to the house those scientists were working in. They combed through the place. They have shipped all the documentation and animals—-dead and alive—-back to Washington for further examination. They also detected a trace of radioactivity in the place." Simms said.

Regan stopped blowing on his hands to keep them warm long enough to glance over at Simms with a quizzical expression. "Radiation?"

Simms nodded. "Yeah. Not sure where it was coming from, but it was there. Not enough to be dangerous to casual exposure."

"Anybody have any theories what they were doing with radioactive material?" Regan asked.

Simms shook his head. "Not as yet. They might be able to piece something together once they have had more time to go through what they pulled out of there."

"So, what's our plan? You want to try to get into the sheriff's office," Regan waved a hand towards a building just up the street, "and see this 'werewolf' thing?"

"I'd like to, but I am inclined to think Sheriff Haines isn't likely going to be receptive to us showing up on his doorstep." Simms said staring across at the police station.

"Well, we have jurisdiction here." Regan said.

Simms nodded. "I know. And we'll use it if we need to, but for the time being let's not exercise that. If the sheriff has the...'werewolf' in custody and he can keep him there then that takes one creature off our list of immediate tasks, but there's still something else out there and our two scientists that we need to round up for us to focus on."

"Yeah." Regan said with a sigh. "I'm not sure how we're going to catch that other thing. At least not without soliciting the sheriff's help on that. We probably will need some manpower to catch that thing."

"Yeah. At some point we will likely need to pull rank on Sheriff Haines and get him on board." Simms acknowledged.

"Well, in my opinion the sooner the—-" Regan started. Simms reached out and grabbed Regan's arm and pointed towards the Sheriff's Office.

"That guy. The one in the shadows over there. I caught a glimpse of his face. He looks like one of our missing scientists." Simms said.

Regan stared at the figure for a moment. The headlights of a car illuminated the man's face briefly. "Does kind of look like it. Should we ease over there and grab him?"

Simms shook his head. "I'm afraid if the other scientist sees us do that we might never find that one. Let's wait. See if this one will lead us to his partner."

They waited for a few minutes and finally the guy moved off down the street. Quietly and casually they moved along on the opposite of the street following the guy. The man only went a short distance away before ducking into a bar. Simms and Regan crossed the street and eased into the bar as well.

The bar was fairly busy. It seemed that with the recent attacks by the 'werewolf' drinking had become one of the most popular pastimes in Mountain Crest.

Simms and Regan stood for a moment just inside the door and scanned the patrons. It took only a moment to recognize the guy they were following sitting down at a table with his fellow rogue scientist.

Simms waved to a table not far from the door and the both of them took a seat.

"As soon as they leave here and get some place quiet we'll take them." Simms said.

"And if they don't leave or go some place quiet?" Regan asked.

Simms just looked at Regan.

Regan nodded. "Right. We'll just take them anyway."

A waitress came by and Regan was about to order a beer, but a look from Simms and Regan waved the waitress off.

They watched the two scientists talk intently for a few minutes and then get up to leave. Once the scientists were out the door Simms and Regan were up and following them out.

Outside the street was busier than usual. People who apparently had been hiding out in their homes in fear of the creature terrorizing their town now seemed to feel a need to escape their self imposed hiding places.

"Where did all these people come from?" Regan asked.

"They all think they're safe now that the creature was caught." Simms said.

Regan glanced up and down the crowded street. "Uh, I don't see them."

"Damn it. I don't either." Simms said.

They stepped off the sidewalk and into the street looking in both directions.

"Damn it." Simms said again.

"Well...?" Regan left the question hanging.

"This way." Simms said with an irritated wave. They crossed the street looking up and down it to try to catch a glimpse of the scientists. They stood for a moment watching the people wandering through the streets.

"Let's try this way." Simms said. They headed up the street. They had moved a couple of blocks which put them further away from the couple of bars that the people seemed to prefer in Mountain Crest and there were fewer people around. At the corner of the main street and an alley they stopped.

"I don't think they went this way." Regan said.

"I agree. Let's—-" Simms stopped. "Did you hear that?"

"I...thought I heard something, but..." Regan listened carefully.

Both of them turned slowly and looked down the alley. It was dark and they really could see next to nothing further than a few feet in front of them. There was, however, the distinct sound of something moving around coming from somewhere deeper into the darkness ahead of them. There was also a sound that strongly resembled a very throaty growl.

Simms and Regan exchanged a quick wordless glance and both of them pulled out their .45s. With a slight nod Simms took a step forward into the darkness of the alley. Regan followed. They hesitated just a few feet in waiting for their eyes to adjust to dark of the alley.

Slowly they eased forward again. The sounds coming from somewhere ahead of them suggested that whatever the thing was back there it didn't seemed to notice them or just didn't care.

As they got closer they could in the dim light of the alley make out a hulking shape rummaging around among some metal trash cans. They couldn't see the thing well enough to know if this was the four legged creature they had seen earlier, the 'werewolf' that was supposed to be in the jail or yet another heretofore unknown creature.

Suddenly there was a quick movement on the part of the creature and in doing so it sent a trash can noisily clanging further down the alley. It was hard to tell what the thing was doing, but both Regan and Simms felt certain it was looking at them. They had dealt with enough creatures now as agents of the OSO to have developed an instinctive sense when something big and deadly was actively watching them.

Then things happened very fast. In an instant the thing was nearly on top of them. It seemed to veer slightly to its left towards Simms. At what was truly the very last second Simms ducked down and to his right. A deadly swipe passed close by primarily because Simms moved as fast as he possibly could and that was only enough to separate him from a large paw full of claws to pass within inches of his head.

Simms swung his right arm up under his left and fired off a shot at the thing. He heard a shot from Regan and also heard it ricochet off the brick wall high above him. An instant later Simms and Regan were left standing in a dark alley staring at each—-alone.

"Did you hit him?" Regan asked.

Simms shook his head. "I don't think so."

"Maybe I did." Regan said.

"I don't think so." Simms said.

"How do you know?" Regan asked.

Simms brushed a few pieces of brick dust out of his hair. "I'm pretty sure you wounded the wall above me."

"Oh." Regan said.

The two of them turned and walked back out to the main street. They had barely taken a couple of steps when there was a scream from somewhere up the street behind them.

"What the hell?" Regan asked.

"Our friend from the alley, maybe." Simms said as they both turned and started running back down the sidewalk. They had backtracked a short distance when people began streaming out of a couple of the bars ahead of them and filled the street.

Frustrated, the best Regan and Simms could do was follow behind the crowd. The people gathered outside of the Sheriff's office. They saw the Sheriff appear at the door and say something to some of the people in the crowd. Simms and Regan couldn't hear what was being said. Before the two of them could push through the crowd and talk to the Sheriff they watched him move off down the street with a group of men. They were moving fast.

"Do we run after them?" Regan asked.

Simms sighed. "No. Let's take a look inside."

They walked into the Sheriff's office. There was no officer at the desk. From the next room where the cells were they could hear people talking quietly. They ducked through the door.

An older man looked up at them from within the jail cell. The woman standing next to the man also stared at them.

"Who are you?" The man asked.

"We're with the Office of Scientific Operations." Regan said.

The man kneeling next to a body on the cell floor just stared at them with a blank expression.

"You can't be in here." The woman said firmly.

Simms stepped closer and held out his ID. "Actually, we can."

The woman stared at the ID, but it was obvious it meant nothing to her.

"Technically, I think we can be anywhere." Regan added.

"Who says?" The man asked.

"Uh, President...Eisenhower." Regan held up his ID as well.

The man looked at the woman and she back at him. They shrugged.

"What do you want? I'm kind of busy here." The man turned back to examining the body.

"The Surgeon General sends his regards." Simms said.

The man stopped and turned to look at Simms. "Oh. You are who they sent?"

"We are." Regan said with a nod.

"Ah. Well, that's different." The man stood up. "I am Dr. Gilchrist. Oh, but I guess you already knew that. This is my assistant, Amy Standish."

Simms and Regan nodded to the two of them.

"So, what happened here?" Simms asked waving towards the bodies.

"Well, it appears these two individuals somehow gained access to the prisoner who...well...was in his other state." Gilchrist said.

"Other state?" Regan asked.

"He was a wolf. A two legged wolf." Amy said.

Simms and Regan exchanged a glance.

"The 'werewolf' creature?" Simms asked hesitantly.

Amy just nodded.

"It killed these two individuals. The wounds are consistent with the other murders." Gilchrist said. "What they were doing in here I can't say."

Simms stepped closer and looked at the nearest body. The dim light had made the face of the body clear enough to see very well.

"Damn." Simms said.

"Oh." Amy said.

Simms glanced over at Amy. "Sorry."

"You recognize the man?" Gilchrist asked.

Simms glanced over at Regan and gave a slight nod. He looked back at Gilchrist.

"I do. He is a scientist. A man, along with his partner, which I assume is that body," Simms pointed over at the other body in the corner of the cell, "which we were sent here to apprehend."

"These are the men that did this to Duncan?" Gilchrist asked.

"Who's Duncan?" Regan asked.

"The werewolf." Amy said.

"That is what we believe, yes." Simms answered.

"So, this 'werewolf' got away then?" Regan asked.

Gilchrist nodded. "Yeah. I'm afraid so."

"They've gone off to catch him again. Well, I think they might kill now." Amy said with a clear note of sadness in her voice.

"Are you here for Duncan too?" Gilchrist asked.

"We are charged with neutralizing threats to the general public." Simms said.

"So you'll kill Mr. Marsh if you catch up with him too, right?" Amy asked.

"We can't have...dangers like this just roaming about the countryside." Simms said.

Gilchrist shook his head slightly. "That's the problem with the government these days. No compassion. Duncan Marsh is a victim here."

"Maybe, but he's a victim that is killing people." Regan said.

"But that's not his fault." Amy said.

Simms sighed. "I'm sorry, but fault is irrelevant at this point. We have one task here and that is to stop the killings. This Duncan Marsh has to be stopped. Whatever that takes."

"And the other thing." Regan said.

"What other thing?" Gilchrist asked.

"There's another creature out there besides this Duncan Marsh guy." Regan said.

"What?" Amy asked.

"There seems to be something else out there as well. We were going to ask these men about Marsh and the other thing, but that's not going to happen now." Simms said looking down at one of the bodies.

"These men?" Gilchrist glanced down at the body in front of him.

"These are the men responsible for these creatures." Regan said.

"Why? What were they trying to do? How did they...?" Gilchrist just stared at the mangled body that lay in a weird twisted position on the floor of the cell.

"We don't know." Simms said. "But we have seized their laboratory and all its contents. Hopefully from that we can determine exactly what they were doing and prevent it from happening again."

"Almost." Regan said.

Simms glanced at Regan. "Almost?"

"We have almost all of the laboratory's contents." Regan answered.

"Oh, right." Simms said with a nod. "Well, we should probably get going to catch up with the Sheriff's party."

Simms and Regan started to leave when Simms stopped and turned back to Gilchrist.

"Doctor, if you could do us a favor and let people in Mountain Crest know that even if the Sheriff catches Marsh there's still something else out there and to be on their guard."

Gilchrist nodded. "Sure. We can do that."

Simms and Regan walked out of the Sheriff's office and into the street. There were growing sounds from off in the direction that the Sheriff and the crowd had moved. Simms and Regan waited for a minute and out of the darkness from down the street people were streaming back into town.

As one of the people passed Regan nodded to him. "Hey, what's going on? Did they already capture the werewolf?"

The guy looked at Regan and shook his head. "Too dark. Can't see a damned thing out there. Sheriff says we have to wait until morning to search for the monster."

Regan glanced at Simms. "Now what?"

Simms shrugged slightly. "Not going to be easy to track either of those creatures in the dark. Too many clouds tonight for the full moon to help us. Guess we wait too."

They trudged back through the slush of the street towards their hotel.

6

In the dim early morning light Regan sat at the restaurant sipping hot coffee. Again he was waiting for

Simms. What few people were in the place spoke in subdued voices. They had thought the night before that their nightmare was over. The monster that had been terrorizing them was finally caught. But Regan knew what they did not. That even if Duncan Marsh still resided in the jail it was likely there would still be more killings.

Simms walked into the restaurant and sat down across from Regan. He pushed a few strands of brown hair off his forehead.

"So, what did the boss have to say?" Regan asked.

Simms glanced over at Regan. He knew that the Director would not have been amused at being referred to as 'The Boss'.

"He said we are to verify that both creatures are either killed or securely locked up." Simms said, but the tone of his voice clearly suggested there was more.

"I'm...not sure these people are capable of catching these things. Certainly not that four legged one. Or, for that matter, keeping them locked up in that jail. Its hardly a high security facility." Regan said.

Simms nodded slightly. "There's a team coming."

"A cleanup team?" Regan asked.

"Yeah." Simms said. "Well, a retrieval team anyway."

They were silent for a moment.

"Ah, they want the bodies. Right. Autopsies." Regan nodded. A frown crossed his face. "Not sure how Marsh's family might feel about that."

Simms looked out the window for a moment. "Yeah. Well, that's not our concern. Or job is mitigation."

Regan nodded slowly. "Right."

The waitress filled a cup in front of Simms with coffee and waited to see if they wanted to order food. Simms shook his head and the waitress walked away. Simms drank his coffee down quickly and pulled out a dollar and laid it down on the table.

"We should get going. We've got...some work to do." Simms said.

Regan finished his coffee. He knew what Simms was saying. Their job did not always required them to be active participants in the termination of a threat. When they did end up in those situations it was typically in the heat of the moment when their lives were in serious danger. In this case, with this Duncan Marsh guy, it felt a little like going out to perform an execution. He was quietly hoping that the Sheriff and his posse would get to Marsh first and, well, solve the issue for them.

As they walked out into the street they saw a large band of men moving out of town. They appeared to be following the tracks of the werewolf in the snow.

"Well, do we just follow the crowd?" Regan asked.

Simms shook his head a little. "I don't think so. Maybe we'll get lucky and they'll take care of Marsh and we can try to find the other creature. Let's see if we can find any tracks from where we last saw the four legged one."

"Sounds like a good plan." Regan said honestly. He would prefer to leave Marsh to the others. The second creature clearly did not seem like it was in any way human.

The Sheriff and his followers were heading east along the road out of town. The last time Simms and Regan had seen the other creature it was a furry blur disappearing between a couple of houses to the south. Not far beyond those houses a heavily wooded ridge rose up giving that side of Mountain Crest a lovely backdrop.

Simms and Regan made their way between the houses and began scouting around in the yards and the property beyond looking for tracks. The tracks of this creature, which they had seen before, were pretty distinct. Additionally, the snow captured everything that moved in a primitive portrait of the past night. It didn't take them long to find something.

"There." Regan pointed. A wide padded print in the snow. There was no doubt what made it.

Simms nodded and they began following the prints that led further out of town along ridge. They moved steadily for a short while until they heard a gun shot somewhere below them on their left.

They exchanged a look. More shots followed.

"Could this thing have doubled back?" Regan pointed down the slope. "Down there?"

Simms shrugged. "Maybe. Let's see what's going on."

They moved carefully down the slope in the snow. As they worked their way along more gun shots echoed through the woods. They reached the edge of the forest and below them they could see a bridge and stone wall that seemed to be a small dam holding back a lake.

“Is that Marsh?” Regan asked. They saw a furry creature in a man’s suit hanging on the edge of the small dam. It looked as though he might drop into water below.

“I think it is.” Simms said.

The creature climbed back up on to the dam. Along the nearby bridge was the sheriff and the members of the town that had accompanied him. They continued to fire at the creature that was once Duncan Marsh. At the end of the dam was a massive rock along the shore line not too far below where Simms and Regan stood.

Simms and Regan watched as the sheriff and the others opened fire on Marsh again. Three more shots hit him and he fell back on to the rock. From their vantage point it was difficult to see Marsh clearly, but they could tell that something changed in Marsh’s body as he lay there.

“Did...he just physically change?” Regan asked in amazement.

Simms hesitated. “I’m...not sure. Too far to be sure.”

They watched the scene for a few minutes longer and then quietly made their way back up the slope to the ridge top. They circled around to try to pick the trial back up again of the other creature.

“I’m not seeing it.” Regan finally said in an exasperated tone.

Simms sighed. “Me either. Its the afternoon sun. Its melting some of this snow. The prints were here, but they’ve faded now.”

Regan shook his head. “I’m not sure how we are going to find this thing.”

“Yeah.” Simms said. “We’re going to need help.”

“Sure. With one phone call we can have a whole battalion up here searching, but that’s going to be hard to explain to these people. They were already edgy about Marsh. Now what do we tell them? There’s another creature out here and, who knows, maybe more.” Regan said.

“God I hope not.” Simms replied. “No, we can’t call in the cavalry on this one. Maybe just a few hand picked locals. Starting with the sheriff.”

They made their way back into Mountain Crest just in time to spot the sheriff further up the street walking into his office.

“That’s right. I’m having him brought into your office.” The sheriff was talking to someone on the phone as Simms and Regan walked in. The sheriff gave them a curt nod.

“I’ll stop by a little later on.” The sheriff hung up the phone. He stared at Simms and Regan for a moment.

“So, as you can see we have handled this on our own.” The sheriff said.

“About that.” Regan said. “It...seems that Marsh was not the only creature those doctors conjured up.”

Haines looked at Regan as if he were speaking some foreign language. "I don't know what you are talking about. This problem has been resolved."

"Not entirely." Simms said. "There's something else out there."

Haines stared at them in silence for a moment. Then he shook his head. "No sir. I have heard of no other incidents other than those involving Duncan Marsh. As far as I'm concerned this whole matter is finished."

"I assure you it is not." Simms said. "And we were hoping to enlist your help in tracking this other creature down."

"Another creature?" Deputy Lauter stopped as he was walking past them.

Haines waved off Lauter's question. He looked at Simms. "Unless you can bring me some proof of this other creature, this whole matter is over."

Simms glanced at Regan. He knew they could make a phone call and have the sheriff ordered to help them, but that would only piss Haines off even more. It was unlikely any cooperation they forced the sheriff into would be limited at best.

"May I suggest that you and your deputy at least remain vigilant. In the event that we are correct about this other creature." Simms said.

Haines sighed. He graced Simms with a sour expression. "We are always vigilant when it comes to the safety of the citizens of Mountain Crest." He stared at Simms.

Simms nodded slightly. “I don’t doubt your capabilities, sheriff. We will endeavor to find you your proof.”

Haines turned away and Simms and Regan walked out of the station.

“Well, that was pointless.” Regan said.

“Maybe.” Simms said.

“Maybe? He’s not going to lift a finger to help hunt this thing down.” Regan said.

“Not right now, but the thought is in his head now. Hopefully it will keep him on the look out—-just in case.” Simms said.

“So what now?” Regan asked.

“I need to let the Director know that even after we eliminate this second creature this area will probably need to be monitor for a while. Just in case there are more of them out there somewhere.” Simms said.

“Alright, well, I’m starving. I will get us a booth at the diner.” Regan said.

Simms nodded and they parted ways. A short time later Simms emerged from the hotel after having briefed the Director. He turned and headed in the direction of the diner when he came to a stop. Regan and another man were rapidly approaching.

“This Mr. Wells.” Regan said as an introduction. “He has a farm not far out of town. Seems he has been losing some of his sheep to what he thinks are wolves.”

Wells nodded. “Never been this bad before.”

“What do mean?” Simms asked.

"They're torn apart. The sheep. Like they was shredded." Wells said.

Regan stood behind Wells and his expression clearly indicated what he thought the cause the sheep kills were.

"Did you tell the sheriff?" Simms asked.

Wells nodded again. "I did, but he just said that he was too busy right now to worry about regular old wolves."

"I think its worth taking a look." Regan said.

Simms nodded. "I agree." He looked at Wells. "Show us your place."

"OK." Wells started to turn to head back down the street they had walked up and then hesitated. "Who'd you guys say you was?"

"The Office of Scientific Operations." Simms answered.

Wells stared at Simms with a blank expression.

"We're government agents." Regan said.

Wells' face lit up. "Ah, gotcha. OK, G-Men, follow me."

They followed Wells back to his farm. They all stood in the gravel drive.

"Up there." Wells pointed past an old barn towards a meadow that sloped up towards the forested side of another ridge. "That's where I keep finding them. Dead."

"You think whatever is killing your sheep is up in those woods?" Simms waved towards the trees.

Wells half shrugged. "Maybe. Or higher up. In the caves."

"Caves?" Regan asked.

Wells nodded. "Yup. There's some caves in the rocks up there. Just past the tree line."

Regan sighed. "Well, ready for another hike?" He looked at Simms.

Simms stared out at the far trees and then higher up where, near the ridge top, some rock outcroppings were just barely visible.

"That's up there a ways." Simms turned and looked at the afternoon sun. "By the time we get all the way up there we're going to starting to lose light."

Regan nodded slowly. "True. So I guess its first thing in the morning."

"Looks like it." Simms turned to Wells. "We'll be back in the morning and check it out."

Wells grunted. Regan got the sense that Wells didn't really believe they would return. Simms and Regan headed back to town.

7

The sun was still just an orange glow on the other side of a ridge to the southeast as Simms and Regan sat in the diner drinking coffee and waiting for the waitress to return to take their order.

"I was wondering..." Regan started, staring down at his coffee.

Simms waited. "Just...in general or was there something specific?"

"Oh, sorry." Regan said looking up. "Do you think we have enough firepower to stop this creature?"

"I thought about that as well, but a .45 has pretty good stopping power for a flesh and blood creature." Simms said.

"Well, not all the creatures we've encountered." Regan said.

"Well, yeah, not something as big as a building." Simms admitted. "But this thing isn't that big. Anyway, I don't think the caliber of our guns is the issue. Its the speed of this thing that worries me. Won't matter what weapon we bring along with us if we can't hit the damned thing."

Regan was silent for a moment and then looked at Simms again. "That did not bolster my confidence at all. Now I have two things worrying me."

"Yeah." Simms said.

"It was another one." A voice from the booth next to theirs could be heard.

"Another one?" A second voice asked in a shaky tone.

Simms and Regan perked up and looked at one another. Regan turned slightly towards the booth behind him.

"Yeah, sheriff said it got that sheep farmer." The voice continued.

In the span of a heartbeat Simms flipped a dollar on to the table and he and Regan were heading out the door of the diner. They made their way over to the sheriff's office, but no one was there.

"Let's go." Simms said waving towards where their car was parked. They drove as fast as the slushy roads allowed them out to Wells' farm. When they pulled into the gravel drive they saw the sheriff's patrol car. Haines stood next to his car talking to Deputy Lauter.

Simms parked next to the sheriff's car and they got out. Haines' expression was clearly different than it was yesterday.

"Gentlemen." Haines said as they walked up. "It...seems I owe you an apology. You tried to warn me, but..."

Simms waved off the sheriff's words. "We are anxious to end this nightmare as well. Is...Wells dead?"

Haines hesitated. "Did you know him?"

"We met him yesterday. He told us about his sheep. We came out to see if it was connected to this second creature." Regan answered.

Haines sighed and looked down at the snowy gravel. "Yeah. He told me about his sheep too. I just didn't take it seriously—-and yes, Wells is dead. Looks like something was trying to get into his barn where he had his sheep."

Simms nodded solemnly. "I guess maybe we should have a look."

"I don't know if you want do that." Lauter said. "It ain't pretty."

"We've seen some pretty dreadful things before." Regan said.

"I don't know. Mr. Wells is really torn apart." Lauter said.

Regan looked at Lauter. "Ever see what happens when a twenty ton prehistoric creature steps on a person? Or what happens when a giant ant cuts a man in two with its pincers?"

Lauter turned a little white. "Uh..."

Even Haines seemed a little shocked. "Oh, that was you guys, I mean, fighting those things?"

"Its a part of the job." Simms said.

"Whoa," Lauter said, "your job sucks."

Regan sighed. "Yeah, that's what everyone says."

They walked over to the corner of the barn. There was a lot of blood. Not a lot of Wells. Haines and Lauter hung back a little.

"We need to kill this thing now." Regan said. His voice carried a bit of emotion.

"Yeah." Simms said coldly.

From behind them came Haines' voice. "Did Wells tell you anything about the thing that was killing his sheep?"

Simms turned back to Haines. "No, but we've already seen it."

"Is it another...werewolf thing, you know, like Duncan Marsh?" Lauter asked.

Regan shook his head and turned away from Wells' body—-or what remained of it. "No. Its...some kind of four legged creature. Like a giant dog, but a hell of a lot meaner."

"Wells thought it might be hanging out in some caves up there." Simms pointed up towards the ridge top.

Haines nodded. "I know those caves. Some of them go in a ways."

"We're going to head up in that direction and see if we can find any sign of this thing." Simms said.

"I can get some men together here in 30, maybe 40 minutes." Haines said.

"We're going to head up there now. You guys can follow us on up." Simms said.

Haines shook his head. "I don't think that's good idea. If that thing is as dangerous as you say it is," Haines glanced over in the direction of Wells' remains, "you better wait for the rest of us."

"The sooner we find this thing the quicker we can kill it. Follow us as soon as you can. If we find it, you'll know it." Simms said.

"Man, that seems crazy dangerous to me." Lauter said.

Regan shrugged. "Its what we do."

Simms and Regan walked past the spot where Wells was killed and moved up across the sloping meadow towards the trees. Before they were even close to the trees they had pulled out their guns and checked them.

They wound their way up through the trees for a while. The further they went the steeper the slope got and the slower they moved. Neither one had spoken after entering the trees.

They stopped to catch their breath. Simms glanced at Regan.

"Something is bothering you." Simms said.

Regan shrugged and looked back down through the trees. "I don't know. Wells, I guess."

Simms waited.

"If we had gone after that thing yesterday, I don't know." Regan said.

Simms nodded slightly. "Yeah. Maybe. No guarantee we would have caught up with this thing."

"I know." Regan said. "We've seen a lot of people die over the years and most of the time there really is nothing we can do about it, but sometimes, you know, the simplest choices we make can make a difference in someone living or dying."

"Yeah." Simms said. "But we make those decisions based on what we know at the time. Hell, if we'd known that creature was going to come back last night to Wells' farm we would have just stayed there and waited for it."

"Yeah, I know." Regan said. "Still, it wears on me sometimes."

Simms nodded. "It wears on all of us, but since, in this new age of scientific wonders, there doesn't seem to be an end to the threats that keep appearing all we can do is keep doing our job. Despite the innocent people that lose their lives because of things like this, we still make a difference."

Regan was quiet for a moment. He sighed. "OK. I guess I've got my breath. I will stop being philosophical and get back to work."

Simms nodded. "OK. Let's go kill this son of a bitch."

Regan held his gun up. "Lets."

A little further on they moved out of the treeline. From here on up it was all rock. The sky was cloudless, but the air up here was crisp and cold.

It was quite steep here and they had to move next to each other because as they moved through the loose rock that millennia of erosion had dropped from higher up they regularly sent chunks tumbling back down the mountain. It would have been very dangerous for one of them to be below the other.

Finally they reached solid rock that required them to do some occasional climbing up on to ledges and zigzag across the rock.

"Hey, over here." Simms pointed just ahead of him.

Regan leaned back to look past Simms. "Is that the cave?"

Simms shrugged. "Not sure if its *the* cave, but is *a* cave."

They moved forward and the area in front of the cave became wider. They stood side by side at the cave entrance.

Regan stepped back a little, went down on one knee and took aim at the cave entrance. He nodded to Simms.

Simms eased closed to the entrance and listened. He heard nothing. He moved close enough to push head into the shadow of the cave.

Regan waited and then he could tell from Simms' body language that he seemed to be leaning in get a better look at something.

"What is it?" Regan asked in a whisper.

Simms' body seemed to relax. "Less of a cave and more of a hole in the wall. It goes in about eight feet and then dead ends. Nothing there."

They moved further along the wide rock ledge. As they slowly walked the steep slope dropping off to their right actually was increasingly less steep. Another ridge line at an angle married into the one they were on a short distance ahead.

"There's another opening just up here." Simms said.

Once again they stood outside the entrance. Simms peeked in. "This one's a genuine cave."

They pulled out flashlights and slowly crept into the shadow of the cave. Their flashlights danced around the inside of the cave. It was obvious that the speed with which this creature could move prompted them to scan around the inside of the cave as quickly as possible. As a result, the sharp angles of the walls and rubble along the floor of the cave created wild and dancing shadows all around them.

Simms held a hand up back towards Regan. He had frozen in place. Regan stopped and tensed up.

Simms crouched down and slowly turned back towards Regan. He whispered. "I think there is something ahead of us."

Regan listened intently. After a moment he heard something as well. A faint rustling.

The cave at this point was fifteen feet wide. Simms waved at Regan indicating they should each get closer to opposite walls. Regan nodded and carefully moved to his left. Simms slid to the right. They both moved very slowly forward.

They had crept another 10 feet when a distinct growl came from somewhere just around a slight bend in the cave ahead of them. They stopped and waited. Nothing.

A moment passed. Simms made a small motion with his hand towards Regan and they eased forward another few feet. Suddenly there was a loud sound that seemed like it was part snarl and part scream. There was blur of motion for just a moment a short distance in front of them. Before they could fire at the thing both of their flashlights lit up what was clearly a mountain lion.

The mountain lion hissed at them and then in an instant it bounded past them out towards the dim light that marked the cave's entrance.

"Shit." Regan said.

"Yeah." Simms said.

"Well, I don't think our creature is in here." Regan said.

"Not if that mountain lion was here. I doubt they would have made good roommates." Simms said.

They made their way back out of the cave warily watching for the mountain lion. Outside the mouth of the cave they saw no sign of the mountain lion. It was long gone.

They moved further along and a short distance ahead they came to another crack in the rock face that served as another cave entrance. This was obviously the largest cave they had found so far. They moved slowly into the cave.

"Bigger." Regan said. "Much bigger."

"Yeah." Simms said. "Looks like it has side tunnels. I think we are going to have to check each one of them out."

"Remind you of something?" Regan asked.

Simms nodded. "Yeah. Not sure if I would rather be hunting giant ants or this thing."

"Well, these," Regan held up his gun, "wouldn't have done us much good against those ants."

"Not sure how effective they are against this creature." Simms said.

"Nice pep talk." Regan said.

"Sorry." Simms said. "I guess, we should just do this systematically. We'll start on the right and work our way around."

They moved down the first tunnel. It narrowed quickly not far into it. They reached a point where there was only enough room for them to go in single file.

"This is not a good formation." Regan said talking quietly towards Simms' back.

"Not a lot of choice." Simms said. "Just don't get too excited and shoot me."

"So, I should wait for it to eat you first and then shoot it?" Regan asked.

"Can't say I like that option much either. OK, fire at will, but try to aim for fur." Simms said over his shoulder.

They only managed to go a little further before Simms stopped.

"Dead end." Simms said. He turned around and Regan did the same. They retraced their steps until they were back out in the main cave.

They moved to the next tunnel. It was wider than the last one. There were small nooks and crevices that appeared along each side as they moved down it. They gave these small avenues only a quick glance and continued down the primary path.

They stopped when Regan inadvertently kicked something and skidded forward with a clatter. Regan shined his flashlight on it.

"A bone." Regan said.

Simms turned and looked around. "There's more up here."

"That seems...oh shit. What the hell is that?" Regan brought the back of his hand up in front of his nose.

"Yeah. That's...strong. I think its coming from..." Simms took a couple of steps forward and shined his flashlight at something. "...that."

Regan stepped up closer to Simms and stared down at the thing. It was clearly the shredded remains of something. It had been mostly eaten.

"One of Wells' sheep?" Regan asked.

"I'm going with a goat." Simms said.

"Whatever. I think we're getting—-" Regan stopped. The sound choked the words off in his throat. It was a deep growl.

Simms and Regan looked at each other. They exchanged an "Oh shit" look. It wasn't just the nature of the sound that worried them. It was the direction the sound came from.

The growl came again. And again, from behind them.

Slowly they turned around and they could see some kind of shape in the shadows back along the tunnel they had already come through. Neither of them directly pointed their flashlights at the shape. They both seemed to have the same idea that the glare of the flashlight might trigger the thing to charge.

The creature eased forward enough to be illuminated by the glow of the flashlights. It was a hideous looking thing. Like some distorted cross between a dog and a wolf.

"Not enough distance." Simms said quietly.

"Yeah." Regan agreed. There was only a short distance between them and the creature. At the speed this thing could move they would each get, at best, one shot off before it was on them. Even of both of them hit the thing they still harbored some doubt if that would stop it.

Both of them slowly backed up trying to gain as much firing distance as possible. The creature just watched them. It seemed to know that it was blocking their exit.

As they moved they had to be careful. Their feet were shuffling backwards through an assortment of bones, loose rocks and a few other, softer, things that they preferred not to think about.

As they gained a little distance the creature, almost casually, moved forward maintaining the distance between them. They backed further, but a short distance deeper and their heads found the ceiling brushing against them. It was obvious they had gone as far back as they could. This was it. They would have to fight this thing right here. In a cramped corner of a dark stinking little cave.

Simms and Regan exchanged a quick side glance at one another. This was as bad a situation as either of them could recall being in. Slowly they crouched down in preparation.

"On 3." Simms said softly.

Regan drew in a deep breath. "Yeah."

"1." Simms said. "2."

Before Simms could finish the creature let out a snarling sound and leaped forward. Both of them fired and both hit the creature. To their pleasant surprise the creature stopped and staggered backwards. It was still standing, but it hesitated, as if gauging how badly it was hurt.

A moment passed and, as they watched, the creature almost seemed to be regaining its strength. As if, in rapid fashion, every second that passed it was absorbing the wounds it had taken and its body was repairing itself.

"Shit." Regan said softly.

The creature shook itself slightly and then clearly tensed up in preparation for another charge at them.

This time there was no count. The two of them started firing repeatedly. Not all of their shots found their mark, but several did. The creature again staggered back, but it still stood after multiple bullets struck it. A moment more passed and the thing spun around and disappeared back down the tunnel.

Simms and Regan stood in silence. They were surprised that they were able to drive it off and then puzzled at how the damned thing could still be alive. Let alone still move at such speed.

"Damn." Simms said. "After it."

They both bolted back down the tunnel.

"How is that thing still alive?" Regan asked.

"I don't know." Simms answered.

"Maybe it can't be killed." Regan said between breaths.

"If its alive it can die." Simms said.

They had turned into the main cave. They really had no idea where the thing had gone. It could have just ducked down one of the other side tunnels, but they just assumed it was exiting the cave. If they were wrong the thing would end up behind them again.

As they rounded a corner they could see the entrance of the cave just ahead. They both skidded to a stop. They had heard something, but they were unsure what it was. It took just a moment to recognize the sounds of men yelling. And then things got crazy.

They heard guns firing. Lots of guns. An instant later bullets began ricocheting into the cave. Both Simms and Regan drop to the floor of the cave. Bullets twanged all around and above them.

Outside the cave they heard above the din of the guns a wild scream. It was a painful scream and was followed by silence. The guns were quiet.

Simms and Regan peeked over at each other.

"You OK?" Simms asked.

Regan nodded. "I think so."

They got up and slowly eased to the cave entrance. They were met with a welcome sight. Sheriff Haines, Deputy Lauter and a good size group of men stood, guns ready, staring at the bullet riddled body of the creature.

In amazement the group stood over the body as it slowly faded from some kind of ferocious creature to a German Shepard.

"Well I'll be damned." Lauter said quietly.

"Yeah." Regan said.

As the group walked back down the mountain Simms managed to draw Sheriff Haines back a little.

"Since we seem to be able to account for all of the killings that took place here, I think we can assume there are no more of those things out there." Simms said.

The sheriff nodded. "I hope so."

"I think for the sake of the general public it would be best if what has happened here, well, remains quiet." Simms said.

Again the sheriff nodded. "I agree. Let's just put this behind us." He hesitated. "But...how do we know what created these creatures couldn't be duplicated somewhere else?"

"The OSO has taken steps to insure that any work those scientists were doing is secured." Simms said.

"I don't think that kind of science is useful to mankind." The sheriff said.

"Doesn't seem like it." Simms agreed. They continued on in silence.

Later, after leaving Mountain Crest, Simms and Regan stopped by the house that had served as the lab for Chambers and Forrest. Marcus had told them the matter had been taken care of and there was, in fact, no house remaining. They stood in front of the flattened still smoldering ruins and listened to the quiet forest all around them.

"Its oddly peaceful here." Simms said staring out into the forest.

"Yeah, you know, when there's no mutated monsters running around trying to rip you apart." Regan said.

"Yeah. That does detract from the beauty of it." Simms said.

"A bit." Regan said.

They stood for a minute more listening to the birds.

"Well, we have more work to do." Simms said.

Regan sighed. "Yeah."

They turned and walked away.

K McConnell

Declassified file: #177

Commonly referred to by the public as "The Creature Walks Among Us".

1956

1

"You wanted to see me sir?" Thomas Wayne, an agent with the Office of Scientific Operations, the OSO, asked as he walked into the office of Marcus Edmonds, the Director of the OSO.

"Please." Marcus said pointing to the upholstered chair directly in front of his desk.

Wayne, a tall, lean man in his early thirties with black hair and a serious look to him, took a seat.

Marcus was staring down at several sheets of paper that lay on his desk. He seemed to be trying to decide something and after a long minute looked across at Wayne.

"It would seem that we may have to revisit a past issue." Marcus said quietly.

"What issue would that be?" Wayne asked.

"Two years ago you and Agent Wyatt attempted to stop this 'Gillman' in Florida." Marcus said.

Wayne perked up a little. "Has there been another sighting of the thing?"

Marcus sighed. "We're not sure. There are rumors circulating in south Florida that the creature is alive in the Everglades."

"Only rumors? We've heard rumors on and off about the creature ever since we lost sight of it in central Florida. Why are these rumors any different?" Wayne asked.

Marcus nodded slightly. "I understand, but there is more. The FBI has been watching a Dr. Barton, a biologist and gifted surgeon, for a while now. Barton has been doing what we would refer to as fringe scientific research."

"Fringe science?" Wayne asked.

"Yes. The kind we frown upon. Unsupervised and unethical in nature. He seems to have substantial financial backing and has a facility just outside of San Francisco." Marcus said.

"OK...what does that have to do with our Gillman in Florida?" Wayne asked.

"Barton is in Florida. He has gathered several other scientists together and hired a boat. The FBI has recorded conversations of Barton indicating that he intends to hunt down and capture an incredible half man half fish creature currently in the Everglades." Marcus explained.

"Hmm, that does sound interesting." Wayne nodded.

Marcus slid a piece of paper across the desk to Wayne. Wayne looked at the sheet of paper.

"The Vagabondia III." Wayne read from the paper.

"Yes, the boat Barton has hired for his hunt. On that sheet is the basic information we have from the FBI. I think you and Agent Wyatt should head down there immediately. We need to watch this closely. If Barton is right and the creature is indeed in the Everglades we need stop that thing once and for all. Also, I believe we have watched this Barton long enough. I want him brought in along with any and all of his research work." Marcus said.

"OK, but, well, Agent Wyatt is already in Florida, um, on a vacation." Wayne said.

"Vacation?" For a moment Marcus' expression suggested that he had never heard of the word vacation.

"Yes sir. With his girlfriend. Wanda." Wayne said.

"Ah, yes. Miss Klemp." Marcus nodded slightly. "Well, that cannot be helped. You will need to go to Florida and collect Agent Wyatt and get after Barton."

Wayne nodded and stood up. "OK."

Marcus leaned over to the intercom and flipped a switch. "Jennifer."

"Yes sir?" Jennifer, Marcus' secretary answered.

"Are Agent Wayne's travel arrangements complete?" Marcus asked.

"Yes sir." Jennifer said.

Marcus looked at Wayne and gestured towards the door. "Get this damned thing. Whatever it takes. We can't let this creature roam freely if its still out there."

Wayne nodded curtly. "Yes sir. Whatever it takes." Wayne turned and walked out.

It was cold and rainy as Wayne made his way to his small apartment on the edge of DC. He threw together the usual small bag of items that most agents carried with them with the basic essentials for being on the road. He looked around the room. It was gloomy and had the musty smell of disuse. He stood there for a moment or two longer than any practical need would require him to. He felt the quiet pang of something deep inside of him. It wasn't the first time he had felt it, but he had never felt if before his partner Agent Wyatt had come back from a vacation two years ago with Wanda.

She had followed him back to Washington DC from Indonesia and they had been living together in a more spacious apartment since then. Wayne thought Wanda was fine, but the OSO did not encourage its agents to build a personal life. Their job required them to regularly risk their lives and having friends and family somewhere would only eventually create a distraction. A distraction that could easily result in people dying.

Still, the thought of having to share something other than confronting monsters and trying not to get yourself or others killed with someone special held a strong attraction to a man as he got older.

Wayne sighed and dismissed the feeling. With deliberate steps he walked out of the apartment.

His flight to Miami was, as usual, uneventful. He stepped out of the plane and as he stood at the top of the steps leading down to the tarmac he shaded his eyes from the warm afternoon sun. An impatient sound from behind Wayne prompted him to make his way down the steps and on into the airport.

A car was waiting for Wayne at the airport and he wound his way through the city to the hotel Jennifer had given him that Wyatt was staying at. Wayne thought about Jennifer for a moment. She was very efficient at her job and he appreciated that. He pushed any other thoughts of Jennifer out of his mind as he parked the car.

Wayne walked into the lobby and after a moment of looking around headed towards the front desk. Before he reached the counter his eyes caught sight of Wanda. There were large glass doors opposite those at the front of the hotel that led out on to a wide and sunny veranda complete with tables, chairs, umbrellas and a nice view of the ocean.

Wayne moved across the lobby and through the glass doors. As he did so he saw Wyatt sitting at the same table. Wanda spotted Wayne first and her expression darkened. It wasn't that she didn't like Wayne, they were on friendly enough terms, it was the fact that Wayne was here and what that implied.

Wanda clearly said something to Wyatt and he partially turned in his chair to look up at Wayne as he came to the table.

"I am desperately hoping you are here because you missed me." Wyatt said.

"That would be wishful thinking on your part." Wayne said.

"Thomas, we're on vacation." Wanda said.

"I did mention that to the Director, but, as you know, he seemed unfamiliar with the word vacation." Wayne said with a trace of a smile.

"Everyone needs vacations." Wanda said without a smile.

"What's going on?" Wyatt asked.

"The Gillman." Wayne said.

Wyatt sat up in his chair and looked more intently at Wayne. "They found him?"

"Shit." Wanda said. She knew ever since Wyatt and Wayne had tried to catch that particular creature two years earlier that Wyatt had been somewhat obsessed with the thing. Wyatt's degree in Zoology had only increased his interest in the discovery of such an animal. Unlike most of the monsters that the OSO hunted this one was not the intentional or unintentional product of humans tinkering with science.

"Maybe." Wayne said. "There is a group of scientists led by a Dr. Barton that seem to believe that the creature is in the Everglades. They have hired a boat and are moving out, even now, into the Everglades to look for it."

Wyatt stood up. "And we are going after them?"

"Yes." Wayne said.

Wanda stood up. "Then I'm going too."

Wyatt and Wayne both looked at Wanda.

"No." Wyatt said. "It will be dangerous."

"No." Wayne said. "Its against OSO rules."

"Yes." Wanda said, crossing her arms.

Wyatt and Wanda stared at each other.

"I need a story to write." Wanda said. "Its what I do. I write stories and sell them. I haven't had anything to write about in, well, you know, a while."

Wyatt was about to say something, but Wanda's intense stare seemed to suck the words out of him before he could actually speak. He knew she was desperate for something to work on and he knew from their past experiences that she wasn't new to being in danger.

"Civilians are not allowed on our missions." Wayne said.

Wyatt glanced over at Wayne. Wayne returned the look. They both knew that the rule had been violated before. Not by them, but other agents.

"I'm...supposed to send you back to DC." Wayne said looking at Wanda.

"I'm not going back." Wanda said flatly.

Wayne looked at Wyatt. He could see that Wyatt was not about fight Wanda on this.

"I am not authorized to force you to go anywhere." Wayne said with a half shrug.

"Good." Wanda said.

"Your bags, sir."

All three of them turned to see Copi standing behind them with Wyatt and Wanda's luggage.

"How...?" Wyatt started.

"I saw Mr. Wayne come into the hotel, sir and it seemed obvious we were departing." Copi said. He was an older man with dark hair and the tanned skin of the people of Indonesia where Wyatt had first met him. He had been general handy man around the institution that Wyatt and Wanda had found themselves in while trying not to get eaten by several different prehistoric creatures.

After Wyatt had returned to Washington DC Copi had shown up at his door one night. The two of them had struck up a trust and friendship which was why Wyatt had told him in Indonesia that Copi would always be welcome. Copi, though, could never seem to shake old habits and acted much more like a personal valet to Wyatt and Wanda which Wyatt was never completely comfortable with.

"Mr. Copi." Wayne nodded to Copi. He had only met the old man a couple of times.

"Mr. Wayne." Copi said with a slight bow.

"Wait, did you say 'we'"? Wayne asked Copi.

Copi nodded. "Of course, sir. I go where Mr. Wyatt and Miss Wanda go."

Wayne looked skeptically over at Wyatt.

"As I have told you in the past, Mr. Copi is a handy man to have around when things get...tough." Wyatt said with a shrug.

Wayne shook his head slightly. "The Director won't like this." He waved his hand around encompassing both Copi and Wanda.

"Well, if you remember correctly, you and I on our own did not have much luck at stopping that thing. An extra gun might be useful when the time comes." Wyatt said.

Wayne sighed. "Whatever."

"Great. So its a party then." Wanda said with a smile.

Wyatt shot her a glance that said "Shut up".

Wanda smiled back at Wyatt and shrugged.

2

The car wound its way down a road that seemed to be going nowhere. Tall grasses, scrubby brush and occasional palm trees flickered past the open windows. The afternoon sun beat down and made everything brighter than it should have been.

Wyatt looked over from the passenger seat at Wayne. "Still no air conditioning?"

Wayne only briefly glanced at Wyatt. "These are company cars. They are, for budget reasons, the very basic models."

Wyatt dangled an arm out the window to feel the air ripple past. "You know, I think this is the same damned car we had two years ago."

Wayne ignored him.

Wyatt looked back at Wanda in the back seat. She was sweating and made a face that indicated she was being cooked alive. Copi, sitting next to Wanda, stared out the window and seemed oblivious to the heat.

Wyatt sighed. "I am seeing more water around us."

Wayne nodded slightly. "We are on the edge of the Everglades. We probably have about 15 more miles before we get to the town."

"And that's where we think Barton and his friends are?" Wyatt asked.

"Yeah. Somewhere around there. We're about two days behind him so its hard to say how far ahead of us he is." Wayne answered.

"I guess I did not realize that the Everglades was navigable without one of those air boats." Wyatt said.

"This part is. At least, that's what I have heard." Wayne said. He turned on to another road where the pavement was not completely intact.

They rattled around in the car for a little while longer before mercifully arriving into a small town along what looked like a river, but Wyatt knew there was a lot more water out there than the open flow that stretched along one side of the town.

They all stood just outside of the car which was parked in front a small restaurant right along the water.

"You said we were supposed to meet the guy here?" Wyatt asked.

Wayne nodded. "Inside. He told an FBI agent some time back about sightings of the creature. I am hoping he has had a sighting of Barton as well."

Wanda looked at Wyatt. "Still standing in the sun." She said with a smile. She had met Wyatt in Indonesia standing in the hot sun on an airport tarmac.

Wyatt smiled at her. "And still hunting monsters."

They walked into the restaurant which was only slightly air conditioned, but it was still much better than standing outside. There were only a couple of people working in the restaurant and about three patrons scattered around at different tables.

One person stood up when they walked in. He was an older man with a somewhat grungy look to him. It was a look, however, that many of the people seemed to sport. This was not a thriving community.

"Are you the G-Men?" He looked at Wayne and Wyatt and then questioningly at Wanda and Copi.

"We are with the OSO." Wayne stated.

"The what?" The man shifted his weight. His overalls were ragged and the T-shirt underneath was long over due for the cleaners.

"The Office of Scientific Operations." Wyatt said, realizing after the words were out that it was not much of an explanation.

The man stared at them for a moment longer clearly not comprehending what they had told him. He shrugged. He waved at the chairs around the table. He sat in one of them.

Wayne, Wyatt, Wanda and Copi took seats that coincidentally all ended up being on the other side of the table from the local man.

"Raney." The man said.

Wyatt glanced out the front window of the restaurant, which desperately needed cleaning.

"Uh, no. No rain." Wyatt said.

"Gerry Raney." The man said looking at Wyatt as if he was an idiot. "Its my name."

"Oh, sorry." Wyatt said.

"OK, Mr. Raney, you told the FBI you have seen a creature around here?" Wayne asked.

"Don't know." Raney said.

"You...don't know if you saw the creature here?" Wayne asked.

"Don't know who they was. They were just G-Men." Raney said.

Wayne sighed a little. "Right. So you saw something?"

"Seen the thing twice." Raney said.

"OK. Can you tell us what you saw?" Wayne asked.

Raney nodded. He pointed towards the far wall. "It was just down the channel. That way. There's a dock down there. I fish off it sometimes."

"And you saw something unusual while you were fishing?" Wyatt asked.

Wanda was sitting next to Wyatt and started scribbling notes down in a small notebook.

"Yup. It was about sunset. That's the good time for catchin' things in the channel. I was doin' pretty good and then the fish just runned off." Raney said.

"Runned?" Wanda said staring down the page in her notebook.

"That's what I said. Runned." Raney looked at her.

Wyatt waved at her to be quiet.

"So, what happened?" Wayne prompted.

"Then I seen it. The back of something. Kinda like a gator, but that weren't no gator. Seen a lot of them and that wasn't one." Raney said.

"You're sure?" Wyatt asked.

"I just told you I was." Raney said indignantly. "Besides, its head came out of the water and that for sure weren't no gator head. It had a face. Like a man's face, but not a man."

"What happened then?" Wayne asked.

"I just stared at it. Then it looked at me. That's when I figured I better get outta there. So I dropped my pole and runned back up along the trail back here." Raney said.

Wanda sighed. She whispered. "Runned. The Queen's English please."

"Your secretary is mighty touchy." Raney said looking at Wanda.

Wyatt quickly turned to Wanda and saw her face reddening.

"Secretary? All women are not—-" Wanda started.

Wyatt reached an arm across in front of Wanda and pulled her closer. "Not now." Wyatt said in her ear.

"You said you saw the creature more than once." Wayne said to Raney.

Raney watched Wyatt and Wanda for a moment and then turned to Wayne. "I seen it again two days later."

"Where was that?" Wayne asked.

Raney pointed in the opposite direction of where the dock seemed to be. "Over by Jimmy's Service Station. That was at night. Jimmy has one of them big lights. Its on all night. The monster just walked right out into the light. Then he crossed the road. He didn't see me. I didn't make no noise."

"That's when he came after me."

Everyone turned to look at a woman that had been sitting two tables away. She had stood up walked closer to where they were sitting. She was dressed in some kind of frock with very faded flowers on it. She was round with aging red hair that was curled by the humidity and not from any attempt to make a fashion statement.

"Aint' nobody goin' after you, Winona." Raney said with a level of disgust.

"You shut up, Gerry. That monster tried to get me. He wanted me for something." Winona said defiantly.

Wyatt tried not to ask the question, but it came out anyway. "Why do think he was after *you*?"

"Cause he stole my underwear and runned off." Winona said pointing a finger at Wyatt.

There was a pause. Everyone seemed to be trying envision some scenario that included those words.

"Your...underwear?" Wayne said trying not to make that sound like a question.

"Yup." Winona said nodding vigorously.

"He physically torn your underwear off?" Wanda had stopped writing and stared at the woman. Skepticism was in her voice and her expression.

Winona gave Wanda a nasty look. "No, girlie, no man or monster better be trying to touch me in those areas."

"Indeed." Copi said quietly.

Wyatt shot a glance at Copi and gave a slight and quick nod.

"The damned thing stoled my underwear off the clothes line." Winona said. "Put it right on his head, he did."

"He put your underwear on his head?" Again Wayne seemed to be articulating his disbelief rather than asking Winona for confirmation.

"Yup." Winona nodded.

There was another moment of silence.

"Wait," Wyatt said, "so the creature came through your yard. You had clothes hanging out on the clothes line. The creature went through the hanging clothes and your underwear happens to get caught on it."

Winona hesitated. "I guess. But he must have wanted it cause he runned off with them when I screamed."

"Doubtful." Copi said.

Again everyone glanced at Copi briefly.

"That's what happened. Don't care what your Injun says." Winona said.

"Right." Wayne said. He looked back at Raney. "Have you seen any other people, 'outsiders', coming through here recently?"

"You mean that big boat?" Raney asked.

"Uh, yeah, the big boat." Wayne said.

"Two days ago." Raney said. "Came here and filled up at Jerry's station. Then went on."

"We...need to get a boat." Wyatt said.

Wayne nodded. "Yeah. Couldn't arrange one ahead of time. Didn't know where we would need to be departing from."

Wyatt looked at Raney. "Anyone around here have a boat we can rent for a few days?"

Raney looked skeptically at Wyatt. "You mean for you all?"

"All of us." Wanda said firmly.

Wyatt glanced at Wanda and then back at Raney. "All of us."

Raney rubbed the back of his neck. "Only boat big enough round here would be Bigsby's."

"Where can we find this Bigsby?" Wayne asked.

Raney shook his head a little. "Bigsby ain't the friendliest guy in town. Specially when it comes to gov'ment guys."

"Well, we can talk to him anyway. Where can we find him?" Wayne said.

Raney shrugged. He waved a hand in a vague direction. "Just up the road. Bout a half mile. Got a place right on the channel. Red roof. Can't miss it."

Wayne stood up. Wyatt, Wanda and Copi did the same. They headed for the door.

"Good luck." Raney said with a snicker.

"Well, he was lovely." Wanda said when they were outside.

"Just a citizen." Wayne said. "Their tax money pays our salaries."

"Maybe." Wyatt said looking around. "But I don't think any taxes are coming out of this town."

"Yeah. Maybe so." Wayne said.

They got in the car and drove a short distance up the only road in the town. Wayne slowed the car as they approached a shabby house that was almost hanging over the water of the channel.

"I guess that's the place." Wayne said.

"Is that red paint or just rust?" Wyatt asked staring at the old metal roof of the house.

"We'll go with red paint." Wayne said and pulled the car up in front of the house. They all started to get out.

"No." Wyatt said looking back at Wanda and Copi. "Stay in the car."

"But—-" Wanda started.

"No." Wyatt said. "Not sure what we may encounter with this guy."

Wayne and Wyatt exchanged a glance as they stood next to the car. They could hear sounds from somewhere behind the house. Wayne nodded his head towards the right side of the house and then nodded towards the left. Wyatt understood. They separated.

Wayne walked down along the left side of the house. The ground dipped down to the water before it reached the back of the house. Some pylons and an aging wooden walkway allowed a person to walk around to the back of the house.

Wayne stepped on to the walkway and then turned the corner of the house. He didn't see anyone. There some crates stacked up on one side of a dock that extended a short distance out into the channel. To Wayne's right was a some kind of wooden storage locker and there was an assortment of fishing gear scattered all about the place.

Wayne started walking out on to the dock when he heard a loud click and stopped.

"Far enough." A voice said.

Wayne didn't move. "Are you Mr. Bigsby?"

"Never heard of him." The voice said. "But if you even twitch I will blow your head off."

"Just want to ask you about renting your boat for a few days." Wayne said calmly.

"That boat ain't going nowhere." The voice said.

"Something wrong with the boat?" Wayne asked.

"You should be more worried about your head than that boat." The voice said.

There was another click. "You might want to worry a little about your own head."

Wayne recognized that voice. He slowly turned around to see Wyatt holding his .45 up to the back of the head of the man who may or may not be Bigsby. The man was in his mid thirties, unshaven, tanned skin, rough brown hair and a physique that suggested he worked a lot of long hard hours.

Wayne watched the man's eyes. He was clearly wrestling with plan.

"We really are here just to ask you about renting the boat." Wayne said.

The man slowly lowered his shotgun. "Told you. The boat's not going anywhere. Motor's blown."

Wyatt pulled his gun back. "You Bigsby?"

The man looked back at Wyatt. He seemed to be studying both of them. "You're government agents."

Wayne nodded slightly. "We are."

"Figured you guys would show up here one of these days." The man said.

"Why?" Wyatt asked.

The guy shrugged. "Can't hide forever."

Wayne and Wyatt exchanged glances.

"You...think we're here for you?" Wayne asked.

The guy hesitated. "Maybe."

"A big boat came through here two days ago. We need to follow it." Wyatt said.

The man stepped sideways so he could see both Wayne and Wyatt. He lowered the shotgun now so it was pointed at the ground.

"I saw it." The man said.

"Any idea where we can find Bigsby now?" Wayne asked.

The man nodded slightly. "Yeah. What are you chasing that other boat for?"

"That's government business Mr. Bigsby and since your boat is out of commission it really doesn't matter now." Wayne said.

"Just Bigsby. How much can you pay for a trip up river? I charge $200 a day." Bigsby said.

"Thought your boat was broken down." Wyatt said.

"It just got fixed." Bigsby said.

"$200 is a lot of money." Wayne said.

"Gotta cover fuel and food." Bigsby said.

Wayne nodded. "OK. $200, but there's four of us and its still $200."

Bigsby hesitated and then shrugged.

"Its too damned hot in the car."

Wayne, Wyatt and Bigsby turned to see Wanda and Copi walking up to them.

"Women cost more." Bigsby said.

"More what?" Wanda asked eyeing Bigsby.

"He wants to charge more money to take us up the river because you're a woman." Wyatt said, trying to hide a smile. He knew what was coming.

"Really?" Wanda asked stepping closer to Bigsby. "Because it doesn't cost me anything to punch you right in the nose." Wanda held up a fist.

Bigsby looked at Wanda for a moment and then at Wayne. "$200. I'll charge her the men's rate."

It took Bigsby a couple of hours to get the boat prepared, but they were moving up the river before the sun set. Bigsby's boat was not only in good working order, but he assured them it moved faster than the

Vagabondia. It was smaller and did not have to go around some of the shallower places. They pushed through the late afternoon and early evening in an effort to close the distance on the Vagabondia, but Bigsby stopped the boat when darkness settled in. He told them it was too dangerous to move very far or very fast in the dark here.

Not knowing for certain how close they might be to the Vagabondia they dropped the anchor slowly and quietly into the black murky waters. They kept the lights off or used them very briefly when they had to.

Bigsby managed in the dark of the galley to put together a meal for them. They sat around at the stern of the boat which was uncovered and ate, talked quietly and marveled at the intensity of the stars. Without any city lights for a hundred miles the sky was impressive.

Wyatt set his plate aside and looked over at Bigsby. "You said something earlier. You said that the government is a piss poor employer. Sounds like you have had some experience working for the government."

Bigsby took a long drink from his bottle of beer. It seemed like he might be just ignoring the implied question.

"Some." Bigsby finally said.

"FBI? CIA?" Wayne asked.

Bigsby waved them off. "I haven't worked for the government since the war."

"Korea?" Wanda asked.

Bigsby shook his head. "The big one."

"Where did you fight? Europe or the Pacific? What front?" Wayne asked.

Bigsby hesitated again. "Europe. No front. OSS."

"Oh." Wayne said.

"Those were the spy guys, right?" Wanda asked.

"Spies?" Copi asked.

"We did information collection, some propaganda and a little dirty work as well." Bigsby said.

"So I assume you were in the field?" Wyatt asked.

Bigsby nodded, but said nothing.

"What dirty work?" Wanda asked.

Bigsby sighed. "I guess it doesn't matter now. There were a few of us chosen to thwart the Nazis' germ warfare."

"What germ warfare?" Wanda asked. "I don't remember hearing anything the Nazis having any weapons like that."

"Exactly." Bigsby said.

"So you took out a biological weapons facility?" Wyatt asked.

Bigsby nodded. "We did. An underground place in Bavaria. January of '45."

"Wow. I would like to hear that story." Wyatt said.

"Well," Bigsby said, "I'm the only one left that could tell that story. The only one that made it out of there alive. Didn't know it at the time, but we were a last ditch effort to stop them and they neglected to tell us that we would all probably die trying to pull off that mission."

"Ah." Wyatt said quietly.

"I spent the last few months of the war repeating the story of what happened there over and over again. Somehow they had trouble believing that I could have survived. They never sent me back out into the field again. Didn't want to go anyway. They kept me safe and secure at a base in England until the war in Europe was over. Then I was sent State side. A month after the war ended they dissolved the OSS and I was out. Not much interested in telling that story these days." Bigsby said.

"Right." Wyatt said.

"Wow." Wanda said leaning back against the stern of the boat.

Copi sat next to her and nodded solemnly.

Everyone was quiet for a minute or two.

Bigsby lit up a cigarette. "So, what did these guys on the big boat do that you want to catch up with them so badly for?"

Wyatt glanced over at Wayne. Wyatt could just make out in the fading twilight a shrug from Wayne.

"We're looking for...a creature." Wyatt said.

"The one people keep seeing here in the Glades?" Bigsby asked.

"That one." Wayne said. "Have you seen it?"

Though it was hard to see now, Bigsby nodded. "I have. Once. It was swimming ahead of me. Knew right away it didn't belong here. I have seen everything that creeps and crawls in this swamp, but nothing like that. Tried to catch up with it, but it was gone before I got close."

"You don't want to get too close to that thing." Wyatt said.

"I'd believe that. It looked pretty damned big." Bigsby paused. "And you think that creature is on that boat?"

"No, but the men on that boat may know where to find it." Wayne said.

"And when they do?" Bigsby asked.

"Don't really know for sure, but ultimately, that thing needs to be killed. It doesn't belong here and its dangerous." Wayne said.

"That's your job?" Bigsby asked.

"Yeah." Wyatt said.

"Jesus. You guys need to find better jobs." Bigsby said.

"I agree." Wanda said.

Bigsby leaned forward and lit a small lantern that he had set between them. He kept the light turned down low.

Wyatt was about to say something when there was a stirring in the water behind Wanda.

"What the hell?" Wanda said as she was suddenly being pulled to her right and backwards. Something large, wet and strong gripped her shoulder. Instinctively both Wyatt and Wayne pulled out their .45s, but in the tight quarters of Bigsby's boat there was no way they could get a shot at whatever was grabbing Wanda.

There was a loud whack and Wanda was released. Something splashed in the water just behind the boat.

Bigsby turned the light of the lantern up and everyone looked at Copi as he stood next to where Wanda was sitting wiping off her shoulder. Copi stood still holding a long handled gaffe hook that he clearly had just used to hit whatever had a hold on Wanda.

Copi calmly looked back at everyone. "The impertinence of that thing."

Bigsby lifted the lantern higher and Wayne and Wyatt, guns ready glanced over the side of the boat and into the dark water. Nothing stirred.

"What the hell was that? Was that the creature?" Wanda asked. She moved away from the back of the boat and close to the door that led down to the lower deck.

"Not sure." Wyatt said. He looked over at Copi. Copi shook his head slightly and shrugged.

"I am thinking we had better post a watch through the night." Wayne said.

"Agreed." Wyatt said.

4

The night passed without further incident. At first light they were moving up the river again. Somewhere around noon Bigsby stopped the boat.

Wyatt climbed up the short steps and into the bridge. "We stopped."

Bigsby waved out to the slow flowing river ahead of them.

Wyatt looked at the river. It turned slightly up ahead and there continued to be jungle and tall grasses bordering each side.

"I don't see anything." Wyatt said.

Bigsby pointed towards the grasses on the left. "Over there."

Wyatt stared at the grasses and remained puzzled. Then he saw what Bigsby was pointing at.

Wayne came into the bridge. "What's going on?"

Wyatt pointed. "Just over the top of the grass over there."

Wayne looked. It took him a minute to see it. "Is that a boat?"

Bigsby nodded. "The Vagabondia, I would guess. Aren't too many boats big enough out here to be spotted over the grass."

"Can we get close enough to see what they're doing?" Wayne asked.

Bigsby thought for a moment. "Maybe. If we cross the channel. Park up close to the grass over there. We might be able to climb on the roof with some binoculars."

"Hmm, binoculars would have been good to bring along." Wayne said.

Seconds passed and Wayne realized Bigsby was looking at him.

"Oh, you have some." Wayne said.

"Being prepared is an old habit." Bigsby said.

"Right." Wayne said.

Bigsby eased the boat over to the left side of the channel. He made sure the boat made very little noise, but there was little they could do about the alligator that was spooked out of the grass and splashed into the water as they drew near.

Bigsby quietly anchored the boat. He disappeared below deck and then returned with two sets of binoculars.

Wyatt briefed Wanda and Copi on why they had stopped and on being quiet. Afterwards he followed Wayne and Bigsby up on to the roof of the bridge. They determined if they knelt on the roof they could get a decent view of the Vagabondia. Enough of a view, in fact, to ascertain that it was for sure the Vagabondia.

Bigsby used one set of binoculars while Wayne and Wyatt shared the other pair. They watched for a short while, but nothing seemed to be happening.

"Could they have left the boat?" Wyatt asked in a whisper.

"Where? Its all swamp here." Wayne said quietly.

Minutes passed and then Bigsby pointed to the right. Wayne scanned to the right. He looked over at Bigsby with a questioning look.

"Bubbles." Bigsby said in a hushed voice.

Wayne looked at the water's surface. They were several spots where bubbles were rising to the surface.

"Divers." Bigsby said.

Some time passed and then divers appeared on the surface of the water. They moved towards the Vagabondia as a couple of men emerged from somewhere inside the boat to meet them. It was difficult to tell what was happening, but it seemed as if one of the divers was unconscious.

"Is that a woman?" Bigsby asked. He was referring to the person they were carrying back on to the Vagabondia.

"Well, its not a creature." Wyatt said.

Bigsby glanced over at Wyatt. "Yeah. I figured that part out."

They watched for a while, but then the Vagabondia began moving up river. The three of them climbed back down. Bigsby started the engine and, when a safe distance separated the two boats he slowly eased forward. He maintained a discreet distance sometimes letting the Vagabondia out of sight before picking them up again.

"What do you think they're doing?" Wanda asked as she and Wyatt sat in the back of the boat.

"Not sure. Maybe they've found the creature and are following it. Maybe not. Hard to tell." Wyatt said.

"If the find it are you going to kill it?" Wanda asked.

"That's the general idea." Wyatt said.

"As a zoologist aren't you a little tempted to see the thing captured and taken in for study?" Wanda asked.

"I admit I have a certain fascination for the creature, but having watched how that worked out back in '54 and what that thing is capable of doing, I think we are better off studying it after its dead. Its just too dangerous." Wyatt replied.

The sun dropped below the horizon. The shore of the river grew into more jungle and much less grass as they had traveled further up river. The Vagabondia had turned into narrower channel. This made it harder to keep an eye on it and still remain out of sight. When the Vagabondia came to a stop Bigsby pulled his boat dangerously close to the shore. In the darkness they could easily have driven right into some of the trees that hung out into the river.

Wayne and Bigsby watched the Vagabondia from the roof the bridge once again, but nothing seemed to be happening.

Wanda sat on the floor of the boat near the back with a small light on as she furiously scribbled down notes.

Wyatt stared at Wanda for a couple of minutes from the door that led down to the lower deck. Finally he moved closer to her and sat down.

"Hey." Wanda said, briefly looking up.

"Hey." Wyatt said quietly.

After another minute Wanda stopped writing and looked over at Wyatt. "What do you think they are doing over there?"

"On the Vagabondia?" Wyatt asked, his voice seemed distracted.

"Yeah." Wanda watched him.

Wyatt shrugged slightly. "Hard to say."

They sat silently for a minute before Wanda spoke up. "Something's bothering you."

It took Wyatt almost another minute to answer. "Yeah."

"You want to share?" The tone in Wanda's voice indicated that it wasn't really a question.

Wyatt sighed. "I don't know. Something just doesn't feel right."

"Right?" Wanda asked. "What's right? We are secretly chasing some crazy scientists that are trying to catch a monster that has killed who knows how many people and you're going to try to stop them and kill the creature."

"That part doesn't actually bother me. Its what I do." Wyatt said. "This is something else."

"Like what?" Wanda asked.

"I don't know. Just a bad feeling. Never quite felt this before." Wyatt said.

"You've faced monsters before. This one as a matter of fact." Wanda said.

"I know." Wyatt sighed. "But I wish you weren't here."

"You know damned well that I can take care of myself, you know, mostly anyway." Wanda said.

Wyatt hesitated. "I know, but in this business if something goes wrong things can get really ugly really fast. With you here I am thinking far more about how to keep you safe than about how we are going to kill the creature."

Wanda was quiet for a moment. "Yeah. I knew that. I knew I might put an extra burden on you by being here, but I've been thinking some while you've been gone on your last few missions for the OSO and, well, I don't think you realize how hard it is for me to just be hanging out in DC while you are out here dealing with, you know, monsters."

"I...don't want to lose you, but, Wanda, this is what I do and its pretty damned important. This world has become a crazy and dangerous place these days and I believe, sometimes anyway, that we might just be the reason it isn't far worse."

"I know." Wanda said. "I'm not asking you to quit the OSO. But I don't think I can just be the little woman sitting at home. I don't know what that means yet, but, I don't know, maybe there's role for me in this part of your life. Maybe its something we can talk about when we get back."

"OK." Wyatt's voice carried a note of uncertainty, but he reached out and put a hand on Wanda's shoulder which seemed to say that he at least understood some of what she was saying.

"I will be here too."

Both Wyatt and Wanda jumped at the sound. They turned to see the dim silhouette of Copi standing near them.

"Jesus Copi. You scared the shit out of us." Wyatt said.

"Sorry sir. However, I doubt if I were the monster I would have spoken so clearly." Copi said.

"Still scared the shit out of us." Wanda said.

Wyatt looked up at Wayne and Bigsby on the roof. There seemed to be a flurry of whispering going on. Wyatt moved across the deck and climbed up to join them.

"Something's going on. Hard to tell what." Wayne said quietly as Wyatt crawled up next to him. "The light is pretty dim around their boat, but they seem to being putting some stuff in a small boat."

"Looks like they're going to move further up that small channel." Bigsby said.

Wayne looked back at Wyatt. "What do you think? Should we try to take Bigsby's small skiff and follow them?"

Wyatt shook his head a little skeptically. "I don't see any way we can avoid detection if we go in there. Its just too tight."

Wayne sighed. "I agree."

"Well, we're not going to lose them." Wyatt said. "They can't go very far in that small boat. As long as the Vagabondia is sitting there they're still here."

"Yeah." Wayne said. "Still, I'd like to know what's going on."

"Yeah, but it sure looks to me like they're still searching for the creature." Wyatt said.

"Yeah." Bigsby said setting down his binoculars. "They don't have it yet."

A few minutes passed.

"I don't hear their motor any more." Wyatt said.

Wayne shook his head. "I don't either."

A short time passed and they lay on the roof in silence.

"Wait. Do you hear that?" Wyatt asked.

"Yeah. Sounded like gun shots." Wayne said.

"A pistol." Bigsby added.

"We need to get out there." Wayne said. "We'll take the small boat."

"Prep the boat. I'll keep an eye out here until we're ready to go." Wyatt said.

"OK." Wayne and Bigsby climbed back down off the roof. It took them a few minutes to get the boat ready. Wyatt climbed down and they got themselves arranged in the boat. Copi pushed them off and they paddled slowly out in the channel. They crept around the slight bend that separated them from the Vagabondia. They would have to slip past the Vagabondia to get to the small channel. The hope was that there was no one left on watch on the Vagabondia to catch sight of them.

"Wait. Stop. Do you hear that?" Wyatt whispered.

All three sat silently for a moment.

"That's the motor on the small boat." Wayne said.

"They're coming back." Wyatt said.

Without any need for discussion the three of them turned their boat around paddled as fast as they could without making too much sound. As they eased around bend once again they could see the a light steadily creeping out of the small channel.

They pulled up next to Bigsby's boat, tied off the small boat and moved as quickly as they could back up on to the roof.

"Looks like someone is hurt. They're trying to get him on board." Wayne said staring through the binoculars and then handing them over to Wyatt for a look.

"Whoever that someone is, they're pretty damned big." Bigsby said.

"Son of a bitch." Wyatt said.

"Is it him?" Wayne asked.

"By its size, yeah. Has to be." Wyatt said.

"And they're actually taking that thing on to their boat?" Wayne said. "They have no idea how dangerous that thing is."

"Yeah." Wyatt said. "We better prepare ourselves to get over there quickly. For a rescue mission."

5

They took shifts again watching the Vagabondia through the night, but all was quiet. In the dim light of the predawn Bigsby stuck his head in the doorway to the lower deck.

"You better get up here." Bigsby called down.

Wayne and Wyatt were the first ones up on deck.

"Trouble?" Wyatt asked.

"Is it the creature?" Wayne asked.

Bigsby shook his head. "No, worse. It looks like they're moving."

"How is that worse than people screaming and being killed?" Wyatt asked wiping his tired eyes.

"Because there's only one way they can go." Bigsby said.

"Right past us." Wayne said.

"What do you want to do?" Bigsby asked. "If they see us sitting here they'll know we were watching them."

"Right." Wayne said again. "OK, get us going. Turn us around get us as far upstream as you can before they can spot us."

"What are you thinking?" Wyatt asked.

"If they encounter us further away maybe they will just think we are tourists out on a midnight ride in the Everglades." Wayne said.

Bigsby nodded. "About as good a plan as any." He headed up on to the bridge. The motor was running and they were backing out away from the shore in minutes.

Wanda and Copi appeared from below.

"What's going on?" Wanda asked.

Wyatt looked at her. "We just became tourists. Go grab some drinks."

"What should I do, sir?" Copi asked.

Wyatt thought for a moment. "You be you."

"Sir?" Copi asked.

"You'll blend in as the hired help." Wyatt said.

"Ah, very clever sir." Copi said and bowed slightly.

Bigsby had the boat swung around and was making good speed back up the river. They could hear the bigger engine of the Vagabondia, but it had not as yet moved out of the smaller channel it was in.

Bigsby got them up around a couple of bends in the river before they caught sight of the top of the Vagabondia through the trees. He cut the engine so it appeared as though they were just lazily drifting along.

Down on the deck Wayne, Wyatt and Wanda had arranged themselves in relaxed lounging positions, each with a drink in their hand. Copi stood nearby with a tray in one hand and a towel draped over the other arm.

It took another fifteen minutes for the Vagabondia to catch up with them. As it passed Wayne, Wyatt and Wanda all waved happily at the three people they could see standing at the rail watching them. The three people, a woman and two men, tentatively waved back. They seemed to be talking among themselves and then with a shrug they moved on towards the back of the boat and in through a door.

The Vagabondia sailed on. When it was just out of sight Bigsby increased the speed of their boat making sure to remain out of sight, but close enough that they either could hear the Vagabondia or, occasionally, catch sight of it over the tall grasses they were moving through once again.

They followed the Vagabondia for hours. The sun was bright and hot. Finally the day wound down and Bigsby watched closely for the Vagabondia to stop for the night. He didn't want to suddenly catch up with them. That would seem suspicious.

Just before dark Bigsby and Wayne stood in the bridge still keeping an eye on the Vagabondia.

"Huh." Bigsy said.

"What?" Wayne asked casually.

"They're bearing to starboard." Bigsby said.

"OK. So?" Wayne asked.

"The port channel goes back the way we came." Bigsby said.

Wayne stared at the river and the tall grasses around them. It all looked the same to him. "Where does the starboard channel go?"

"To the southwest." Bigsby said.

"And where does that take them?" Wayne asked.

"Well, if they follow it far enough, the Gulf." Bigsby said.

"The Gulf of Mexico?" Wayne asked.

Bigsby glanced over at Wayne. "You know any other gulfs around here?"

Wayne ignored Bigsby. He was thinking. "If they cross the Gulf of Mexico...could that boat go through the Panama canal. I mean, do they let boats that size go through there?"

"Hah." Bigsby said. "You can go anywhere you want if you have enough money and pay the right people. But...why would they want to?"

"Because Barton, the guy we're following, he has a place in San Francisco." Wayne said.

Bigsby nodded slowly. "Then that's probably where they're going."

Wyatt came up on to the bridge and Wayne explained what was happening and what he thought Barton's intention was.

"So the question now is, do we stop Barton before he gets much further." Wyatt said.

Bigsby eyed the two of them. "You thinking of trying to stop that boat here in the Glades?"

"Not sure." Wayne said.

"I am." Bigsby said.

"What do you mean?" Wyatt asked.

Bigsby shook his head. "We ain't stopping that boat with this one."

"Your boat's faster than that one." Wayne said.

Bigsby scoffed. "I could catch him alright, but then what? I'm not ramming him. He'll smash the shit out of us."

They were all quiet for a moment.

"Can your boat cross the Gulf of Mexico?" Wayne asked.

Bigsby nodded. "Long as there's no hurricanes it can."

Wayne looked at Wyatt. "I will need to call the Director, but I don't see much choice right now. If he wants us to stop the Vagabondia then he can call the Coast Guard and we can stop him out in the Gulf of Mexico."

Wyatt nodded. "I agree."

"She's stopping." Bigsby said.

Wayne and Wyatt looked into the distance ahead of them. The dim light now that the sun had just dropped below the horizon made it hard to see the top of the Vagabondia.

"Yeah. Guess its going to anchor there for the night." Wayne said.

"Not a good idea to try to navigate the Glades at night." Bigsby said.

"We need to make sure we are up well before dawn, though." Wyatt said.

"Agreed." Wayne said.

It was early in the morning, though still dark, when Wayne woke Wyatt up.

"Bigsby's up on the bridge. We're going to get ready for dawn." Wayne said.

"Right." Wyatt said and he followed Wayne up to the bridge.

"Can't see a damned thing yet." Wyatt said.

Bigsby nodded in the dark of the bridge. "Yeah. It gets pretty damned dark out here. Should start to see some light in the Eastern sky soon."

They waited about another 30 minutes before the sky began a slow steady gray light that replaced the blackness. Even as the predawn light began creeping across the grasses it was still nearly impossible to spot something that was just barely above the foliage.

Minutes continued to pass.

"I still can't see it." Wyatt said.

Wayne had the binoculars and said nothing.

Finally Wayne started out of the bridge. "I'm going up on top."

Bigsby and Wyatt followed him. They were initially on their knees and then Bigsby and Wayne stood up, each staring through binoculars.

"Shit. I think they're gone." Wayne said.

"Yeah." Bigsby said. "Gutsy captain there."

"You think they knew we were following them?" Wyatt asked.

Wayne shook his head and lowered the binoculars. "Don't know. We need to get going."

"Right." Bigsby said and ducked down into the bridge. The engines fired up and Bigsby got the boat moving quickly. He kept their speed up. Being faster than the Vagabondia they knew they should be able to catch up eventually.

Time passed with no sight of the Vagabondia. Several times Bigsby slowed down to decide on a path forward. There seemed to be endless side channels that appeared along the way.

At one junction Wyatt had to ask. "How do you know which one to take?"

Bigsby glanced over at Wyatt. "I don't."

"What do you mean?" Wayne asked.

"There's no charts for this. Wouldn't do you any good if there were. It changes all the time." Bigsby said.

"How do you know we're going the same way they are?" Wayne asked.

"We don't." Bigsby said. He looked at them and saw their concern. "We're assuming they're headed for the Gulf. So we keep working our way to the Southwest. We either catch sight of them or we both end up dumping out into the Gulf somewhere and we'll need to find them in the open water."

"So, what you're saying is that we just have to get lucky?" Wyatt asked.

"Yeah. Pretty much." Bigsby said.

"Shit." Wyatt said.

6

They pushed on through the day with no sight of the Vagabondia. Bigsby drove into the twilight as far as possible. It wasn't just a matter of not wanting to run aground in the dark while trying to navigate solely with a spotlight on the bow, it became impossible to tell whether the boat was turning into a larger channel or into something small that would dead end.

At the earliest light they were moving again. By early afternoon their surroundings had significantly changed. They were working through channels, some of them frighteningly narrow, of mangroves. It was obvious they were rapidly approaching the Gulf.

They emerged from another narrow channel that, on occasion forced them to cut upper branches of mangrove to fit the boat through, to find themselves staring straight out into the Gulf of Mexico.

Bigsby pointed his boat straight out from the mangroves. They wanted to get as wide a view of the coast behind them as possible with the hope that they might spot the Vagabondia. It was apparent that Nature was not going help them. Dark clouds loomed above them rolling in from the west. Within about 40 minutes a light shower began and worse yet, heavier rain and fog was closing in around them.

Wayne and Copi were on the port side scanning the horizon while Wyatt and Wanda stared out from the starboard side. As the weather engulfed them all hope of spotting the Vagabondia disappeared.

Bigsby cut the engines and came down from the bridge. The others joined him.

"Well?" Bigsby asked looking at Wayne and then Wyatt.

"I'll call the Director." Wayne said. "We're going to have to have the Coast Guard hunt them down."

Bigsby rubbed a hand across his stubble covered face. "They're going to have a hard time spotting them in this." He waved up and towards the west.

"Maybe it will pass soon." Wanda said.

Bigsby shook his head. "Doubt it. Don't think it will be out of here until early tomorrow."

"I guess as soon as it clears they will need to get some planes up." Wyatt said.

"By then they will probably be in International waters. Coast Guard doesn't have jurisdiction out there," Bigsby pointed out.

"Let's see what the Director wants to do." Wayne said. He headed up into the bridge to call in.

Bigsby went up to the bridge with Wayne. The others went below to get out of the rain and increasing wind. It wasn't too long before Wayne joined them below.

"The Director is calling the Coast Guard, but does not think they will be able to catch up with the Vagabondia before it reaches International waters. More than that, he's not sure he really wants to try to stop them at sea." Wayne said.

"Why not?" Wyatt asked.

"He's...concerned about the safety of the Coast Guard guys. He thinks in the close quarters of a boat that creature could be very hard to deal with." Wayne explained.

Wyatt nodded. "Right. That could be...a problem."

"So now what?" Wanda asked.

"Stop them at the Canal." Wyatt said.

"Maybe." Wayne said. "I suggested that, but the Director isn't sure he can do that. There are, I guess, treaties and...well, it could easily turn into quite a circus. If somehow we lost the creature there the

Panamanians would be screaming about us dumping a monster on to them."

"So we are back to what now?" Wanda said.

"Actually, the Director is advocating doing nothing. For now." Wayne said. "Let them get to San Francisco, if they can, and maybe even to Barton's compound. Its outside of the city. It might be a safer place to deal with this."

"So, basically find them if we can and then just follow them." Wyatt said.

"Yeah." Wayne said.

"So, a holiday cruise. I can live with that." Wanda said.

Bigsby took the boat to Key West where they refueled and restocked the provisions. From there they headed south to Havana. They circled around Cuba and stopped in the Cayman Islands. Bigsby's boat could only carry enough fuel and supplies to allow them to stay at sea for a few days.

It took them a while along the Nicaraguan coast to find a place they could resupply, but from there they could reach Colon at the mouth of the Panama Canal.

They had not been tied up at a dock in Colon for more than an hour when an American solider drove up near the dock and appeared alongside their boat. Wayne climbed out on to the dock.

The soldier saluted. "Private Roberts, sir."

"You...don't have to salute me." Wayne said. "I work for the OSO, not the military."

"Oh, sorry, sir." Roberts said, a little confused. "I...have orders to deliver a message to you."

They stood looking at each for a moment.

Finally Wayne asked. "So, what's the message?"

"Oh, right. Sorry sir." Roberts pulled a piece of paper out of his pocket and read from it. "The Vaga...bond...dia passed Fort Sherman 5 hours ago. You are to follow it at a reasonable distance. Your ship..."

Roberts glanced at Bigsby's boat, "uh, boat, has the highest priority through the Canal."

Wayne nodded. "Thank you. Give my regards to men at Fort Sherman."

Roberts looked concerned. "But, I'm not from Fort Sherman. I'm at Fort Randolph."

Wayne sighed. "OK, then don't worry about it."

Roberts looked relieved. He started to salute and then stopped himself. He turned to leave and then turned back again.

"Sir?" Roberts asked.

"Yes?" Wayne asked.

"What's an OSO?" Roberts asked.

"They kill monsters." Wanda called up from the boat.

Roberts looked at Wayne, then Wanda and then Copi. "Really?"

Wayne waved it off. "Sometimes. Thank you Private."

Roberts nodded and headed back up the dock towards his jeep.

Bigsby finished getting the boat resupplied and they headed out of Colon and into the first section of the Canal—-much to the clear anger and frustration of a large French freighter who was next in line.

Once they cleared that section of the Canal they headed south across Lake Gatun. They passed numerous freighters parked in a rough line waiting their passage through the lower part of the waterway. It took them a couple of hours to navigate to the lower end of the lake.

"There." Wyatt said as he and Bigsby and Wayne stood in the bridge watching in all directions.

"Where?" Wayne asked.

Wyatt pointed to the starboard side. "There. Just lost sight of it. Its on the other side of that black and red freighter."

Bigsby throttled the boat down. "So what do you want to do?"

"Stop." Wayne said. "We wait. When they go, we follow."

Bigsby moved the boat off at an angle. When they anchored they could just see the front of the Vagabondia sticking out a little from the bow of the freighter. If the Vagabondia moved they would see it right away.

Wayne got a hold of the Canal authorities and coordinated their plan. He managed to get the Vagabondia a higher priority. They would only have to wait about 12 hours now instead of 36. In addition, once the Vagabondia was underway their own boat had became the next in the queue.

They spent the next 12 hours redecorating. There was a concern that if the crew of the Vagabondia looked back and saw their boat they might recognize it from the Everglades. That would make things difficult. If they knew they were being followed it was likely they would try to run somewhere. As in, a country with no extradition treaty with the United States.

They moved an assortment of boxes and crates that Bigsby had stowed in the hold of the boat up on to the front deck. They couldn't disguise themselves as an actual freighter, but they could look like a small local boat hauling some kind of freight.

When the appointed time arrived, as luck would have it, darkness had fallen. It would be harder for the crew of the Vagabondia to get a good view of them.

Slightly ahead of schedule the Vagabondia began slowly moving towards the southern end of the lake. When it was an appropriate distance ahead Bigsby got their boat moving. Both boats steadily navigated their way through the river, then canal, then river that led past Panama City.

As the night sky began giving way to the gray dawn both boats had begun working their way up the western coast of Panama. With daylight Bigsby had dropped back so that the Vagabondia was just a tiny boat on the horizon. There was less of a concern now of losing Barton and his precious cargo. They knew where he was headed and once they reached US waters the Coast Guard would start providing aerial surveillance.

"What's going on? Why did we stop?" Wayne asked as he stepped up into the bridge. He had left Wyatt and Wanda enjoying a drink on the deck below.

Bigsby pointed ahead of them. "They stopped."

Wayne looked through the binoculars. "Damn. Hard to see from this distance."

Wyatt joined them. "What's up?"

Wayne shook his head. "Don't know. They stopped."

"You think they spotted us?" Wyatt asked.

Bigsby shook his head a little. "Doubt it. We're just a speck on the horizon."

"I have to get higher." Wayne said and left the bridge. He climbed up on to roof.

Wyatt borrowed Bigsby's binoculars and followed Wayne.

"Shit." Wayne said. He was standing on the roof of the bridge, but the waves were rocking the boat and he had nearly fallen over the side already.

Wyatt stared through the binoculars. It was difficult to get a good view of a distant object while rolling from side to side and, even worse, it didn't take long to start feeling seasickness looking through a pair of binoculars in those conditions.

"Whoa." Wyatt said. He lowered the binoculars. "Can't take much of that."

"What the hell?" Wayne lowered his binoculars for a moment as well. "It looks like they are jumping off the boat."

Wyatt did a quick stare through his binoculars. He could see people on the deck staring overboard. He lowered the binoculars again and almost lost his balance.

"You think that creature is loose on their boat?" Wyatt asked.

"If it is we'll have to close in. We have to make sure that thing dies." Wayne said.

"If he gets into the water we might never find him." Wyatt said.

"You think he can survive long out here?" Wayne looked at Wyatt.

Wyatt thought about for a minute. "I honestly don't know. When we were chasing in Florida he seemed to disappear for a while into the ocean, but we don't really know if he was in there for very long. He's a freshwater creature. Seems like saltwater would start to be a problem for him after a while."

Wayne shook his head. "I don't think we can risk it. I think we need to close in and try to kill him now."

Wyatt sighed. "I imagine Barton will try to stop us."

"I know." Wayne said. He was staring again through the binoculars. "Wait."

Wyatt lifted his binoculars. "Looks like they are pulling something into the boat."

"Something big." Wayne said. "If that's our Gillman, and I think it is, he doesn't look to be in good shape. He's limp."

After a few more minutes of watching the Vagabondia started moving again.

"If you guys don't want to end up in the Pacific I would suggest coming down from there." Bigsby called up to them.

Wayne and Wyatt climbed down and Bigsby got the boat moving again.

7

The slow and steady trip up along the west coast of Central America, then Mexico and finally California was tedious. They felt helpless. There was the ever present fear that the creature might simply escape from Barton and his cronies and dive into the ocean where, presumably, they might never find him again.

The Vagabondia docked in San Francisco under cover of darkness. Bigsby was forced to docked their boat further away, but Marcus had already arranged for Federal agents to watch ever move of Barton and his crew. While it appeared as though Barton was quite pleased at getting his people and their prize package on to a truck and up to his compound in the hills above San Francisco they were watched and followed the entire way.

Leaving Bigsby to attend his boat, Wayne and Wyatt, with Wanda and Copi in tow, were met by an FBI agent by the name of Fleming. He briefed them on the surveillance of Barton and drove them in the early hours of the morning to a camp they had set up on hill overlooking Barton's compound. There tents and communications there waiting for them.

Wayne and Wyatt had a good view of Barton's place. Particularly with the high powered binoculars the military had provided for them.

Fleming, a middle aged man, walked out of the communications tent to where Wayne and Wyatt were surveying Barton's house below.

"Just got the word they're on the move." Fleming said.

Wayne looked at Fleming. "Did you say that there were going to be soldiers available to move in here when we need them?"

Fleming nodded. "Yes, sir. There is a platoon on standby from the Oakland Army Terminal. Once you guys have a plan developed we can call them up here and get them deployed."

Wayne nodded. "Good."

Wanda walked up next to them. She looked down at Barton's house.

"So, this is where you're going to kill that thing?" Wanda asked.

Wyatt nodded. "Yeah. This is where that creature's story needs to end."

It was another 40 minutes before they caught sight of the truck, presumably carrying the creature, appeared on the road heading up to the house. A car followed closely behind the truck. They both drove into the open gate of the place and came to a stop. People climbed out of the truck and the car. There were already several men waiting for them armed with rifles.

Wayne and Wyatt watched as the back of the truck was opened and the people stood around and waited.

"What are they doing?" Wyatt asked. "Are they just letting the thing walk around on its own?"

"I don't know. That truck doesn't look like it could hold some kind of water tank for that creature to travel in." Wayne said.

"Yeah." Wyatt said. "Something doesn't seem right about this."

Minutes passed and then they saw it.

"What the hell?" Wyatt said.

"What is it?" Wanda asked standing next to Wyatt. She did not have a pair of binoculars and just stood shading her eyes against the sun staring down the mountain.

"I..." Wayne said. "Don't understand..."

"What? What's going on?" Wanda asked again.

"The...creature looks different. Very Different." Wyatt said amazed.

"What happened to it?" Wayne asked.

Wyatt studied the scene below carefully. "I...think they altered the creature. It looks like something, I don't know, closer to human now."

"Can they do that?" Wayne asked still staring through his binoculars.

"It sure as hell looks like they did." Wyatt said.

"Why? Why would they do that?" Wayne asked.

"I don't know." Wyatt answered.

"They did that on the trip from Florida?" Wanda asked.

Wayne and Wyatt lowered their binoculars and looked at one another.

Wyatt turned to look at Wanda. "I...guess so. That seems crazy to try something like that at sea."

"They must have had to." Wayne said. "I mean, why else would you try something like that on a boat at sea?"

Wyatt nodded. "I guess so."

"Its more than just physical changes." Wayne said was looking through the binoculars again.

Wyatt watched for a minute more. "You're right. When we encountered that thing it acted more like a wild animal. Its seems...almost docile now."

"Yeah." Wayne said lowering his binoculars. "They've got him locked up in a pen. Seems like if he wanted to get out of that he could easily."

Wyatt looked over at Wayne. "I think I saw some electrical insulators on that fencing."

"Ah," Wayne said, "that makes more sense."

Wyatt glanced up at the sky. "Its getting late in the day. If we're going to go in there we probably would want to do it earlier in the day. If, for some reason, that thing gets out during our raid I don't want to lose it in the dark. We're not that far from the ocean."

Wayne nodded. "I agree. We'll make a plan in the morning."

They settled into camp. They could only use the cook stove that had been provided to them. A campfire would have sent up smoke that might have been seen from Barton's place. When darkness fell they sat for a time in the dark center of their encampment. Only the dim light from Barton's compound was visible around them. There was a dull glow in the sky from San Francisco, but nothing more.

It wasn't long before they all retired to their tents. Down the road, the only road that led up here, a couple of miles there was a couple of FBI agents on watch in case anyone left Barton's home.

"Hey!" Fleming leaned into the tent that held Wayne and Copi.

Wayne sat up. "What?"

"Something's happening down there." Fleming said.

"Get Jonathon." Wayne said. He pulled his shoes on and stepped out into camp. Copi appeared a moment later next to him.

"Trouble, sir?" Copi asked.

"Don't know." Wayne said.

Fleming and Wyatt joined Wayne and Copi. They all hustled over to where they could look down at Barton's place.

“I was out here having a smoke.” Fleming said. “Heard some kind of scream.”

“A person or the creature?” Wyatt asked.

Fleming hesitated. “Actually, sounded more like a cougar. I’ve lived out here all my life. Heard it a few times.”

Wayne and Wyatt stared through the binoculars again.

“Can’t see much.” Wyatt said. “The light down there is pretty dim.”

“Yeah.” Wayne said.

“What’s going on?” Wanda asked appearing next to Wyatt.

Wyatt shook his head a little. “Don’t know.”

They watched for a little while.

“Looks like they are hauling something dead out of the pen.” Wyatt said.

“Yeah. You think that thing killed one of them?” Wayne asked.

“I...don’t think so.” Wyatt said. “It...looks like, yeah, that’s an animal. There’s another body. That second one is definitely a sheep.”

Wayne lowered his binoculars. “I think we need to have someone watching the place throughout the night.”

“Yeah. Probably a good idea.” Wyatt said.

“I can watch, sir.” Copi volunteered.

Wyatt glanced at Wayne who nodded an OK.

“Let us know if there’s any activity down there.” Wayne said to Copi.

“Yes, sir.” Copi said and found a rock at the edge of the slope to sit down on. Wyatt handed Copi his binoculars.

The rest of them returned to their tents. They had only a short time to try to back to sleep before Copi was calling out to them.

Wyatt popped out of his tent and nearly ran into Copi. There was a crashing sound from somewhere down the mountain.

“Sir—-” Copi started.

“I hear it.” Wyatt said.

Wayne appeared next to them, Fleming behind him and Wanda emerged from the tent she was sharing with Wyatt. They all moved to where they could see Barton's place below.

"It sounds like all hell is breaking loose down there." Wyatt said.

"I don't think that thing is as docile as you thought." Wayne said. "We need to get down there now."

"Agreed." Wyatt said.

Wayne turned to Fleming. "Get a hold of those agents down the road. Tell them to get up here fast. And contact the Oakland Army Terminal. Tell them to get the soldiers up here as soon as they can."

Fleming nodded and was off at a run.

Wyatt was going to say something to Wayne and then a different thought came to him. He turned to Wanda. "You stay here."

Wanda's face grew dark. "What? This is the story. The story I am here for."

"No." Wyatt voice was firm. "This thing's a killer. I don't want you anywhere near it."

"But—-" Wanda started.

"No." Wyatt said and Wanda could tell there was no changing his mind. He ran back to the tent and returned slipping on his shoulder holster and stuffing his .45 into it.

Wayne and gone back to his tent and did the same. As he was ducking out of the tent he stopped for a moment. He caught sight of the rifle leaning in the corner of the tent. He grabbed it and met Wyatt out in the middle of their camp. They moved to where they watched Barton's house from.

"I say we just suck it up and just head straight down there." Wyatt said.

Wayne looked down at the rugged slope below them. "I agree. It would take us too long to backtrack down to the road."

They went down through loose rock and scrub brush. They made precariously good time getting down to a place just outside the fence that encircled the entire compound. They could still hear the sound of things being smashed coming from somewhere in the house. The lights of the house had gone out just before they reached the fence.

There was a scream. A woman's voice.

"We need to get in there." Wayne said.

"Yeah, but how?" Wyatt staring up at the electric fence in front of them.

"This way." Wayne said and started moving to his right along the fence. Wyatt followed him.

There was another scream. This one was a deeper voice. A man.

"Maybe we should just call out to them to let us in." Wyatt said.

"How?" Wayne asked. "There's no gate here."

"I think its ahead of us if I remember how it looked from up there." Wyatt said. "Let's keep going."

They heard a gun shot from somewhere ahead. They kept going. Ahead there was a sudden light show. Sparks were shooting up from something. By the time they reached the spot there were only a few spots of the smashed electric fence still giving off a few sparks. The pillar on the right side of the wrecked front gate had been toppled.

"Our friend must have done that." Wyatt said.

"Yeah." Wayne said. "That means its free."

They both stared off into the tall brush beyond the destroyed perimeter. From somewhere in the dark they could hear some brush being trampled.

Wayne and Wyatt looked at each other. They had been in this position before. Trying to stop this thing on their own and they had failed to kill it, but they knew that they were not very far from the outskirts of San Francisco.

"I guess its just us." Wyatt said.

"Yeah." Wayne said. His voice carried the doubt they both were quietly harboring.

A moment later the two of them were plunging into the dark brush in pursuit of the creature.

8

It was difficult going through the scrub brush in the dark, but fortunately the gray glow of the morning was rapidly growing. They could hear the creature ahead of them and they could tell that they were moving at a faster rate than the creature was. After a brief discussion they decided to circle ahead of the creature and confront it at the first open place they came to.

It didn't take them long to maneuver themselves into the path of the creature. They weren't sure if the creature could hear their movements, but it didn't seem to react to them if it did.

They had found a small clearing where only brush no higher than their knees was. There was thin fog slowly drifting through the clearing and all around them. They figured they weren't much more than a mile from Barton's place.

Then the brush on the far side of the clearing parted and the creature emerged. It did not stop, but kept walking almost directly at them. It had moved several steps into the clearing and then seemed to catch sight of Wayne and Wyatt. It stopped and stared at them.

Wyatt wondered if its vision out of water was poor. No one moved.

"You think it remembers us?" Wyatt asked quietly.

Wayne shrugged. "Don't know." He held his .45 out in front of him. Wyatt was doing the same.

"Maybe we can just drive it back to Barton's and then wait for the soldiers to show up." Wyatt said.

"That sounds like more luck than we normally have." Wayne said.

"Yeah. Probably so." Wyatt said.

The light of the day was growing fast. The creature seemed to be staring at them as if it couldn't quite understand what it was seeing. Suddenly it seemed to catch sight of something. Wyatt thought it was the guns.

They had only seen the creature lumbering around at Barton's place when they had been watching it, but suddenly it moved very fast. It came directly at them.

Both of them got off a shot that looked like they hit the creature, but it didn't slow down. Wayne, slightly in front, was knocked aside with one sweep of the creature's arm. The rifle went flying off into the grass somewhere.

The creature's left arm glanced off Wyatt's shoulder and then his head. Wyatt saw stars spinning around his eyes and stumbled to his right and down on to the ground. He shook his head to try to clear it. He heard a shot. A .45.

Wyatt finally got back up on his feet. He looked over and saw the back of the creature. It was bent over Wayne. Wyatt knew that was not good. He decided to get up try to put a bullet point blank into the back of the creature's head. He rushed over to it.

Just before Wyatt could position the gun the creature swung an arm back and struck Wyatt in the chest. Wyatt felt like he had been kicked by a mule. All of the air blew out of his lungs and he fell straight back on the ground.

Wyatt lay there trying to suck the air back into his chest. He turned on his side and got up on one knee. He glanced over and felt his stomach clinch. The creature was holding Wayne up with one hand by the throat. He could hear Wayne gasping for air.

Wyatt desperately looked around for one of the guns. While his head was wildly swiveling around he heard two quick shots. Wayne's .45. The creature groaned and dropped Wayne.

Wyatt was still shakily trying to get to his feet as the creature turned and look at him. It took step towards him and reached out to grab Wyatt when a rifle fired and the creature staggered a little. The creature glanced left and then moved off into the brush.

Wyatt stumbled over to Wayne who was not moving. Wyatt glanced up as Wanda and Copi appeared next to him. Copi was holding one of the other rifles from their camp.

Wyatt knelt next to Wayne. Wanda let out a cry and knelt down as well.

"His...his throat." Wanda said quietly.

Wyatt stared at Wayne. Wayne's eyes were open, but it was obvious that his throat was crushed. He was suffocating.

"We...we need to..." Wyatt said his voice was cracking a bit. They were too far from anywhere to get Wayne help before...

Wayne's eyes knew it. He reached a hand up and put it on Wyatt's shoulder. He nodded his head slightly. A moment later his hand slid off Wyatt's shoulder and Wayne stopped struggling to breathe.

"No..." Wyatt said softly.

"Oh my God." Wanda said.

Behind the two of them, Copi stood with the rifle watching the brush where the creature had disappeared.

9

Minutes passed. No one said anything. Finally Wanda could not choke back the tears any further. She began to cry. Her crying pulled Wyatt out of his shock. He stood up. He glanced briefly down at Thomas Wayne, his partner.

Wyatt glanced in the direction the creature had walked off. He turned to Copi.

"Both of our 45s and our rifle are around here somewhere. Find them and watch her." Wyatt pointed at Wanda. "If that thing comes back here you make sure you kill it. Use the rifle."

Copi nodded solemnly. "I will kill it."

Wyatt reached out and Copi handed him the gun he had brought. Wyatt turned and started walking towards the trampled path the creature left.

Wanda jumped up. "No, Wyatt!" She yelled. "Don't. Let the Army kill that damned thing."

Wyatt turned back and looked at her. "They won't catch it in time. I am going to kill that son of a bitch once and all."

"But it could kill you." Wanda pleaded.

Wyatt shook his head slowly. He glanced down at Wayne and then back to Wanda. "No. Not today. I will kill that creature." Wyatt turned and disappeared into the brush. He could hear Wanda crying, but he wasn't going to stop now until he stood over the Gill Man's dead body.

It took Wyatt some time to catch up with the creature. By the time he did they were both down to the shoreline. The creature was about fifty yards ahead of Wyatt. When he spotted the monster Wyatt broke into a run after it.

"Stop you son of a bitch!" Wyatt yelled. He had closed the distance between them to about thirty feet.

Oddly, at the water's edge the creature did stop. It turned to look at Wyatt. Wyatt could see blood running from a couple of wounds.

Wyatt shouldered the rifle, but hesitated. The creature showed no aggression. It just stood staring at Wyatt. Based on what had happened when Wayne and Wyatt had pointed guns at it earlier Wyatt was sure it knew what the rifle was capable of. Still, it just stood there.

The monster's whole story passed through Wyatt's head. It had been living isolated in the Amazon until humans had decided to drag out of there and into the world of men. It didn't ask to abducted, confused, terrified and hunted.

Wyatt knew in his gut none of this was the creature's fault. Once again, like so many of their past encounters, the blame for this lay squarely at the feet of humanity.

The moment passed and the creature turned back to the ocean. Wyatt knew if it got into the water it was likely going to escape and, if it survived, end up killing more people. Still, he was having trouble pulling the trigger. Then Wayne's face seem to float into Wyatt's vision. Pain and anger flooded back into Wyatt.

The creature was now knee deep in the water when Wyatt fired. He hit it in the left shoulder. The creature stumbled slightly, but didn't stop. It wader deeper into the ocean.

Wyatt felt the pressure of not letting this thing get away again. He took a deep breath to steady his thoughts about what happened to Wayne and the consequences of the creature escaping. He took aim.

Wyatt fired and hit the creature square in the middle of the back. This time the Gill Man stopped. It stood for just a moment more and then slowly leaned forward, falling face first into the water. Its body sunk beneath the surface.

Wyatt was afraid the creature was underwater now swimming away. He took a couple of steps forward, unsure what to do. Then he saw the creature's body reappear. It was floating face down.

Wyatt wanted to put at least a couple more bullets into it, but very little of the creature was visible above the water's surface. He was doubtful that, at this range, he could hit it.

The body was now well out into the deeper water. Wyatt just watched. He was trying to see if there was any sign of life left in it. He had to be sure it was dead, but this thing had survived so much already he wasn't sure what it would take to finally put an end to it.

Minutes passed and then Wyatt's stomach sank. He saw it move. He lifted the rifle up to shoot at it again, but he knew that would be futile from here.

Wyatt saw the body move again, but there was something odd about its movement. Wyatt stared at it and then saw it. Just beyond the creature's floating body. A fin. Wyatt recognized it immediately. A shark. A big one.

The fin disappeared and then the body moved again. A jerky movement. Wyatt knew what that was too. The fin broke the surface again and then a second fin appeared. A third fin cut through the water and bore down on the creature's bobbing body.

The gruesome scene playing out in the ocean was familiar to Wyatt. A feeding frenzy. The sharks were making a meal of the Gill Man. Now Wyatt was sure. No one would see this thing alive again.

9

The conference room at OSO headquarters in Washington DC was not large. It held an oval conference table and all eight chairs were occupied. Elliot Simms, the District Chief Investigator sat at one end of the table and next to him was District Investigator Robbie Regan. On Simms' other side was DI Wyatt. Next to Wyatt sat Wanda and then Copi.

Next to Regan was Lieutenant Ridley, the chief communications officer, on loan from the Army. On Ridley's left sat Jennifer, the Director's secretary. Marcus Edmonds sat in the last chair.

They were all silent as everyone involved in the mission with the Gill Man had gone through their version of the story. Jennifer had been taking extensive notes and laying in front of Marcus was an open file folder containing Wyatt's official report.

Marcus had said little during the meeting up to this point. He cleared his throat.

"Well, I guess that covers...that." Marcus said. There was another moment of silence before he spoke again.

"I know this is hard on all of us. None of you here, with the exception of Elliot, has gone through something like this before, but it is a part of the risk in this job, We all know it. But you also know how important what we do is." Marcus said. He was staring down at the folder in front of him, but looked up and around at all of them.

Wanda sniffled a little.

Marcus glanced at her. "I also want to thank Miss Klemp and Mr. Copi for assisting the OSO in this endeavor. What you did in saving

Agent Wyatt's life was very courageous. You have the gratitude of this Agency."

Wyatt reached a hand out and caressed Wanda's shoulder. Copi nodded solemnly towards the Director.

"Though our sacrifice in this case was great let us remember that what all of you did in stopping this Gill Man most assuredly saved many people's lives. Never forget, that is who we are and that's what we are here to do." Marcus said.

"Sir?" Wyatt spoke up. "What do we do now?" He was thinking about how they were always given assignments in pairs. It was generally discouraged for an agent to tackle a dangerous assignment without a partner.

Marcus looked at Wyatt. Whether Marcus understood what Wyatt was asking or why he was asking it, was unclear.

"We are going to keep doing this job. This world keeps getting more dangerous each and every day. It needs us now more than ever." Marcus paused for a moment. "We keep going."

K McConnell

www.kmcconnellbooks.com[1]

kmcconnell@kmcconnellbooks.com

1. http://www.kmcconnellbooks.com/

The Hamlet Mysteries series...

The Hamlet Mysteries 1

To Not Be In Hamlet

Sam MacNeil, part time mystery writer, has returned to his hometown to house sit for his parents as they start a lengthy vacation. What Sam has forgotten while away is the quirky weirdness of the little town of Hamlet. With expectations that he would quietly do his time in Hamlet the discovery of a dead body, clearly murdered, changes everything. Now Sam finds, much to his chagrin, the residents of Hamlet are expecting him to solve the murder. Not only does Sam not want to be involved in it, but the authroities have made it clear his help is not wanted. Was it the angry businessman from Detroit? Was it the shifty handyman the victim worked with? Sam doesn't know, but when killers from Detroit show up the situation is taking a serious and deadly turn. And then there's Becky. An old friend who clearly has more than friendship on her mind. Murder, killers and romance...this is not how this brief stay in Hamlet was supposed to go.

The Art of Hamlet

An old family friend asks Sam to look into a break in at her house. She is an art collector and critic, but nothing has been stolen and the only thing disturbed are some small statues. While it is a puzzling incident Sam doesn't think it is a serious issue, but when a neighbor is murdered and found bobbing in a nearby lake the story is once again taking a dark turn. As usual Sam is not inclined to get involved in a murder investigation, but somehow he seems to be sliding in that direction anyway. In addition, the County Detective seems to have recognized that Sam might be of some use—-regardless of the consequences for Sam. And what of Sam's old classmate, who is now a seemingly crazy hermit, ranting on about terrorists in Hamlet? Is that actually possible? To complicate things even further something is happening between Sam and Becky. Love and Death seem to be chasing Sam through the wacky streets of Hamlet.

Ophelia's Hunt

Sam's women troubles have seemingly tripled. There is Becky and the relationship that Sam has found himself in with her. However, suddenly, there is Callie. Sam's wealthy and wild ex-fiance who has appeared in Hamlet. Is she here to get Sam back? Everyone thinks so—-including Becky. Then there's the beautiful woman named Misty. She seems to have a particular interest in Sam as well. And, of course, there's murder in Hamlet once again. Questions abound. Is the lovely Misty a suspect or a new love interest? Who are the men stalking Callie? How is Sam going explain all of this to an increasingly angry Becky? Why is the County Detective actually soliciting Sam's help? Should Sam be flattered or very careful? With love and murder swirling around Sam how is he going to survive this?

The Hamlet Mysteries 2

The Ghosts of Hamlet

Sam MacNeil, part time writer, is house sitting for his parents in his hometown of Hamlet. The people of Hamlet are far more quirky than Sam remembers from his childhood and he is keen on leaving them behind and getting his life back, but it's those dead bodies that are the real problem. They just keep showing up. Murder in the small town of Hamlet has taken a noticeable uptick since Sam has returned and the residents have taken notice. Sam claims it has nothing to do with him and yet...Now, even worse, the residents are seeing ghosts and they blame Sam for that as well.

Sam may get his chance to escape Hamlet now that his parents are heading home, but can he really walk away without solving the mystery of the ghosts? Will he get away before the "gangsters" from Detroit catch up with him and turn him into a ghost? And what about Becky? He really wasn't planning on a romantic entanglement to muddle things up.

So what do ghosts, gangsters, girlfriends, musk ox and talking cans of beans all have in common? Sam MacNeil and the quirky town of Hamlet, of course.

The Play of Hamlet

It is finally here. The Founder's Day festival in Hamlet. A gala event highlighted by a play depicting the bizarre founding of Hamlet. Sam is not only the star of the play, but also a target for Scanlon and his killers from Detroit. They are determined to finish him off once and for all. But Sam knows they are coming and, with the help of the quirky residents of Hamlet, he has his own plans in the works. What Sam doesn't know is that Scanlon isn't the only killer from Sam's past that is out to get him. Could the biggest day of the year in Hamlet be Sam's last?

The King of Hamlet

The sixth story in the Hamlet Mystery series starts out where most of the stories end up...with a dead body. The trouble is Sam is found standing over the dead body and refusing to explain what has happened. He seems willing to take the fall for the guy's murder, but he is clearly hiding something. His friends are sure he didn't commit murder, but who is he protecting and why? What Sam is not telling anyone is that he is playing a more dangerous game than any of them can imagine. As bodies begin piling up around Sam he is increasingly wondering if he has a guardian angel or has become an unwilling accomplice to the Angel of Death. Once again women and murder are causing headaches for Sam.

The Hamlet Mysteries 3

The Graves of Hamlet

As if the town of Hamlet didn't have enough trouble with dead bodies now, it appears, someone is digging them up in the cemetery. The quirky residents of Hamlet are sure this has something to do with Sam. As usual Sam doesn't really want anything to do with whatever is going on, but when someone tries to make the cemetery Sam's permanent home one dark night it would seem that Sam will need to sort this out—-if only to save himself. To add to the confusion, with Becky out of town, Sam must also figure out who the half naked woman is that keeps showing up on his deck sun bathing. Oh, and who are these other guys that just showed up in Hamlet? The grandson of the recently deceased retired cop who is lying about his real identity and the suspicious looking guy casually asking questions around town about the same dead cop...?

Polonius' Plight

Here's a surprise...there's been a murder in Hamlet—-again. This time, however, Sam is very much intentionally involved. It's the suspects. The guy was found with a gaping shotgun blast to the chest. Like the one in the trunk of Renee's car. Of course the last person to be seen with the murder victim was Jen—-and she seems to have disappeared. And why is Reese, the County Detective looking for Becky and her grandfather's .38? Sam is sure none of his friends are murderers, but to keep any and all of them out of jail he needs to find out who the killer is and fast. To make matters worse, while Sam is trying to solve a murder and hide his friends the Town Council of Hamlet has had enough of Sam and the murders that seem to follow him around. They passed yet another of their many bizarre ordinances. Sam has been ordered to leave Hamlet.

A Portrait of Hamlet

Heidi Stevens, art collector and friend of Sam, has an urgent request. She wants Sam to prove her friend, a famous painter living in Hamlet, is innocent of murder. Sam's not that interested in the task and Becky has forbidden him from getting involved in any more murders. But there's a problem. Someone is very clearly trying to kill Sam—-and maybe Becky too. Is it related to the murder the painter is accused of? Sam doesn't think so, but who is trying to kill him now? And don't even ask what Sam is supposed to do about Bobby Wieters' ax murdered wife. There are too many problems spinning out of control. Sam is deep in it this time in what seems to sadly be normal for the quirky town of Hamlet.

The Office of Scientific Operations

With the conclusion of the traumatic events in 1933 surrounding the shocking affair involving the city of New York and a beast commonly referred to as "King Kong", the president of the United States, Franklin Roosevelt, established the Office of Scientific Operations (OSO). The purpose of the OSO was to monitor and evaluate the level of risk and assist in any manner the mitigation of danger of any and all scientific operations and anomalies. With the rapid pace of scientific discovery this office was given the highest priority and clearance to investigate any potential threats or consequences to the interests of the United States of America.

What follows are the real stories behind the cinematic cover-ups presented to the general public...

Release #1 from the declassified files of the Office of Scientific Operations...

From 1953...

File #153 (commonly referred to by the public as "The Beast from 20,000 Fathoms")

OSO agents Elliot Simms and Robbie Regan, while observing an atomic test in the Arctic, are unwittingly caught up in the release of prehistoric beasts from millions of years of suspended animation in the ice. Now they must help in stopping this new terror as it moves steadily down the east coast destroying anything in it's path.

From 1954...

File #157 (commonly referred to by the public as "Them")

OSO agents Simms and Regan investigate the odd circumstances surrounding a missing FBI agent only to stumble upon a horror in the New Mexico desert and if they cannot find a way to stop it there is a very good chance this could be the end of humanity.

Release #2 from the declassified files of the Office of Scientific Operations...

From 1954...

File #159 (commonly referred to by the public as "Terror in the Jungle")

OSO agent Jonathon Wyatt is pulled off vacation to an island in Indonesia to investigate sightings of pteranodons. The island is not far from the island known infamously as Z Land. It was once the headquarters of Dr. Zeitner whose experiments in genetically manipulating prehistoric monsters terrorized the world in the 1930s before the OSO put a stop to it. Wyatt's job is to determine if these are indeed Dr. Zeitner's creatures, but what he finds is much more deadly. This is no way to spend a vacation—-trying not to get eaten.

Release #3 from the declassified files of the Office of Scientific Operations...

From 1954...

File #161 (commonly referred to by the public as "Revenge of the Creature")

After the capture of an unknown species of half man half fish is brought back to a Florida marine institute, OSO agents Wayne and Wyatt must determine the risk to the American people it poses. When the creature escapes and begins terrorizing the citizens of Florida the risk becomes all too real. Now they must hunt it down and stop it's killing spree, if they can.

From 1955...

File #165 (commonly referred to by the public as "It Came From Beneath the Sea")

OSO agents Simms and Regan are sent out to Pearl Harbor to investigate damage to one of the Navy's most advanced atomic submarines by some kind of giant creature. While the Navy has a hard time believing it, the OSO knows such creatures are real. It soon becomes apparent by the large number of ships being lost that something dangerous is hunting throughout the Pacific. Now, with the creature openly attacking the west coast of the United States Simms and Regan join the fight to stop this thing before the entire Pacific is destroyed by it.

Release #4 from the declassified files of the Office of Scientific Operations...

From 1954...

File #163 (commonly referred to by the public as "The DC Creeper")

On a break from hunting monsters for the Office of Scientific Operations, OSO Agent Wyatt is trying to adjust to a more crowded domestic life. As brutally murdered bodies begin showing up in the nation's capitol, though, this doesn't seem like it is going to be much of a break. The newspapers have dubbed the hulking killer "The Creeper" and it looks like Wyatt is going to have to hunt him down and stop him before Wyatt becomes the next victim.

Release #5 from the declassified files of the Office of Scientific Operations...

From 1956...

File #166 (commonly referred to by the public as "Tarantula")

Agents Simms and Regan from the Office of Scientific Operations, the OSO, returning from the Pacific Coast having just finished dealing with yet another monster threatening the United States are redirected to a small town in Arizona to verify that a large tarantula that has been terrorizing the local inhabitants has been destroyed by the Air Force. With Beka, a woman who insists on tagging along with the intrepid agents—-a clear violation of official regulations—-in tow, they quickly discover that the threat of the giant spiders in the Arizona desert are not over just yet.

From 1956...

File #171 (commonly referred to by the public as "Invasion of the Body Snatchers")

The Office of Scientific Operations, the OSO, has sent agents Wayne and Wyatt out to the small California city of Santa Mira to locate a missing Air Force major, sent to investigate the impact of some meteors, and to understand the meaning of his last cryptic message to Washington. What they find is that, while the city of Santa Mira may look like a quaint place to visit it soon becomes apparent that a missing Air Force major is the least of Wayne and Wyatt's problems. There is something very strange and deadly going on in Santa Mira. Something that seems...alien?

The New Sheriff

Travis Ames, somehow, has developed super powers. Exactly what these powers entail he's not sure. He's still learning how to control his powers, but he's already decided that he should use this new found power to fight crime. And...if he made a little profit along the way, well, that wouldn't be so bad either. But reality has a way of altering the best laid plans. He has quickly figured out he has no idea how to go about crime fighting. And, to make matters worse, he has learned the hard way, his new powers won't protect him from getting hurt or, quite possibly, killed. Can he survive long enough to learn how to use his powers? Can he get an aging detective to teach him how to fight crime? Can he prevent Aubrey, the new girl, and everyone else at work from figuring out what he can do? How long can he keep this up before he makes that one small mistake and ends up dead?

Don't miss out!

Visit the website below and you can sign up to receive emails whenever K McConnell publishes a new book. There's no charge and no obligation.

https://books2read.com/r/B-A-CGLDB-FFQHD

BOOKS 2 READ

Connecting independent readers to independent writers.

Also by K McConnell

Office of Scientific Operations

Office of Scientific Operations - Release #1

The Hamlet Mysteries

The Hamlet Mysteries 1

The Hamlet Mysteries 3

Standalone

A Conspiracy in Blood

Symbiotic Puppets

The Plague

The Club of the Bombastic Few

The Master Switch

Hamlet On A Budget

The New Sheriff

Office of Scientific Operations - Declassified Files (Release #2)

Office of Scientific Operations Release #3

Office of Scientific Operations - Declassified Files (Release #4)

Office of Scientific Operations - Declassified Files (Release #5)

The Hamlet Mysteries 2

Office of Scientific Operations - Release #6

The Hamlet Mysteries 1 - 9

The Trench of the Dead

The Heart of a Monster

Watch for more at www.kmcconnellbooks.com.

www.ingramcontent.com/pod-product-compliance
Lightning Source LLC
LaVergne TN
LVHW091058150826
845673LV00002B/633

* 9 7 9 8 2 3 0 6 3 2 6 3 4 *